Bloody Montana

Clay Burnham

A Black Horse Western

ROBERT HALE · LONDON

Robert Hale Limited
Clerkenwell House
Clerkenwell Green
London EC1R 0HT

Typeset by
Derek Doyle & Associates, Shaw Heath.
Printed and bound in Great Britain by
Antony Rowe Limited, Wiltshire

Bloody Montana

Rafe McDonough needed to survive. The blizzard had come up suddenly and he wasn't prepared for the blinding snow and bitter cold. Then he stumbled across the dead man, shot up-close and personal. Having no choice, McDonough took the dead man's heavy coat and hat to keep warm and stay alive.

But he certainly wasn't prepared for the hot reception on riding into the small, snow-bound Montana town nearby. Looking for a place to wait out the winter, McDonough is mistaken for the dead man. He's shot at, beaten and run down like a dog and it makes him mad. Fighting mad.

Now he's ready to tear up the sleepy town and its secrets to reveal a callous killer who's not finished with murder.

CHAPTER ONE

A pale yellow sun slid behind the distant snow-blued Crazy Mountains and with it went the meager warmth of the day.

The heavy roan shivered once, snorting a blast of steam at the vanquished sun. The night would be a long, cold one and the horse knew it. It was a big animal, better than sixteen hands high, with a thick, hairy hide. It had a sure foot; as sure as any animal could be picking its way across icy, snow-covered slopes. Treachery lay beneath two feet of powdery snow on slick, hidden rocks.

Though the roan chose the trail with sureness, Rafe McDonough held the reins.

Wrapped in a threadbare woolen coat, with a scarf bundled around his bare head, McDonough saw little of what lay ahead as he rocked heavily in the saddle. As so often before, he trusted the horse to find their way safely. He had named it Red because of its coloring – simply Red, and nothing more.

McDonough had bought the roan from old man Tulesko back in South Dakota when the itch to move on came over him. It had been his favorite out of the rancher's cavvy. They had become boon companions, the man and the animal, and had learned to rely on each other when there was naught but lonely prairies and empty mountains for company.

The snow had come up suddenly two days earlier and covered the range with a soft, blinding blanket. After the snow, a Canadian wind blasted down from the north and froze everything. His old packhorse had died, so Red was carrying what little gear McDonough owned. It was a heavy load in this weather, but the animal did not falter.

Coming down out of a low hill, they trudged through a copse of lodgepole pine and another of bare aspen that seemed to shiver in the icy wind. Before long it would be too cold to travel. He had to find shelter, and soon.

Below was another stand of aspen and several outcroppings of snow-covered rock. With luck he would be able to dig into the lee of a boulder and keep out of the wind. There would be enough deadfall scattered about for a fire and the thought of this promised warmth urged him onward.

Then in the waning light of day a spot of liquid red on the virgin hill caught his eye.

The roan spotted it, too, and snorted, disturbed by its meaning.

McDonough dismounted and plodded his way through the snowdrifts. The first red spot lead to another, and then to many more. The wind picked up, shifting to the south, and it began to snow in thick, wet flakes, covering the red spots like a conspirator.

McDonough found the corpse behind a thicket of juniper bushes. There was no hope for the man. Not in this life.

Suddenly, something fluttered in a gust of wind. McDonough turned as quickly as his frozen limbs would allow and saw something black flapping on the bough of a bare ash. It was a hat. A battered, black sombrero and it was stained with blood.

The dead man was tall and strongly built. His face had been beaten recently, his eyes and cheeks bruised, his lips split and covered in dried blood. He lay on his back, his arms spread out at his side. Dead eyes, now milky and vacant, stared up into nothing.

There were four small holes in the man's torso, a line of them from the abdomen up toward the heart on an angle. He wore no coat, which seemed odd to McDonough until he remembered how suddenly the snowy weather had come up. His shirt pocket was torn. His six-gun was holstered, and tied down. A gunman. Yet someone had gotten the drop on him.

McDonough turned away from the dead man and toward an outcropping of rock. A small hollow had formed beneath the bulbous overhang of a round boulder, which was perhaps five feet deep and eight feet wide. Light snow had fallen all around the boulder, but inside the hollow had remained relatively clear and dry.

McDonough picketed Red near the boulder, out of the wind, and quickly made camp. He traveled a lot and knew how to pack light. Often he would leave after a spring round-up, roam loose-footed for a while, and then manage to land at some ranch in time for fall round-up. This year he had left late, enjoying old man Tulesko's company and the fine spread he put out each night at supper. That good food might cost him his life, he thought wryly. He had missed opportunities at two ranches as he worked his way west toward Oregon, and then he had become lost. For a time he had kept to the Yellowstone, but thinking he had found the old Bozeman Trail he headed too far north.

There had been nothing but wilderness for the past three weeks. He had seen no one, not even a stray Indian. It was a lonesome journey, one he did not care to think about now. But a time or two – after a spill from the roan, and later after a run-in with a mountain lion – he wondered if he would just disappear into this empty land never to be seen again.

Despite the loneliness of it, he had always sought out this life. Alone in the wilderness or riding herd on a bunch of lazy cattle, he rarely felt lonesome. He had the land for company. He had seen others on the trail, men like himself, drinking in as he did the sky and the mountains and the rivers. Nodding to them from a blue distance he wondered sometimes what had happened to those men. Whether the land had swallowed them, never to be seen again. It was at those times that he felt a pang in his chest, a reminder of something lost for never having been pursued. The crackle of a fire, the rustle of calico, a whiff of woodsmoke and flour and daffodils. The things any man longs for, if only for a little while.

The snow had stopped. The roan snorted and then whinnied. Surprised, McDonough turned to the animal then paused, hearing another horse return the call. He looked down the slope and saw a dappled gray mare standing off a hundred yards. It was saddled and had brown streaks on its coat. It stood very near the black sombrero, still flapping in the wind.

McDonough approached the animal slowly and took its reins, talking in a gentle voice to calm its fears. The mare seemed to be drawn to the sombrero and to shy from it at the same time.

He did not like to put on a dead man's clothes but he was cold and needed to survive. He took a handful of the new, wet snow and wiped away the dried and browning blood from the flat brim of the hat. The hat was well made, heavy and warm and it fitted his head well enough. The mare snorted when he had put it on, and threw its head once.

At the campsite he picketed the mare next to his roan, removed the saddle, washed the browned blood streaks from its coat, then covered the horse with its saddle blanket.

Finished, McDonough settled back on his heels to enjoy the growing heat of the yellow-orange camp-fire. He let the thaw pulse through his fingers and toes. After a time, curiosity urged him toward the corpse's belongings. The dead man had quite a kit tied to the back of the saddle. Finding a heavy sheepskin coat, sheepskin mittens, and a woolen scarf was a welcome prize. The bedroll was well used but warm. He had a saddle gun, an old Sharps, and a Smith & Wesson .38 Safety tucked under his arm in addition to the gleaming Merwin .44 revolver he wore tied down at his side. There was no food in his kit, little water in the canteen. The dead man had not planned to be gone long; it was either that or he had left in a hurry.

But gone from where?

Lost, McDonough did not know where he might find a town and more sturdy shelter from the winter weather. This dead man had not traveled far, though, so that meant a town or a ranch was near by.

McDonough made a meal of jerky and snow water warmed over the fire. He had run out of coffee more than a week ago. He wore the dead man's coat now, and scarf and mittens, too, and the black sombrero replaced the battered Stetson he had lost more than a week ago. In the morning McDonough returned to the dead man and searched for a clue to where he had come from.

The man's pockets held twenty-two dollars in folding money and a pouch with a dozen gold eagles. In his vest pocket was a piece of paper on which was written *My Dearest Clara*, but that was all. There was no address, no last name.

McDonough took the money and put all of it into the pouch and, along with the letter, stuffed it into the man's saddle bags. He then stripped the man of his guns and gunbelt and put these in the saddle bags as well.

Whoever this man had been he had thought deeply of a woman named Clara. She would want to know about his death and perhaps want his belongings. It was a small thing to do for a dead man; something he hoped someone would do for him one day. Except he had no half-finished letter in his pocket, and no one to send it to if he had written one.

The ground was too hard to dig, and there were no rocks with which to build a cairn, so McDonough shoveled snow atop the corpse, paused a moment in silence, and left.

He rode the gray for a while, testing the mount. It was not as sure-footed as the roan but it had a spirit. It was a cow pony, quick but not meant for climbing. By noon they were out of the hills and onto flat prairie. The mare pranced with obvious relief.

A cold wind bit deeply into McDonough despite the sun's brightness. The weather had cleared so that there were no clouds to be seen anywhere. The sky was an open, icy blue.

McDonough, stiff as a rusty gate, head down, used the heavy black sombrero as a windbreak. By mid-morning the wind had died down enough for him to raise his eyes to the horizon. Misty mountains surrounded him, distant and unreal. He was alone in a great valley so white it made his eyes water to look at it. In the spring, or summer, he would have marveled at this valley. It would be washed in shades of green and gold, flowing with grass and probably crossed by crackling streams. There would be a whispering sound in these fields as a breeze caressed the grass and made it sing. Birds would wheel overhead; the cry of a hawk would echo along the endless plain. But it was winter and there was only the mournful, eerie wail of a frozen wind to be heard.

By mid-afternoon, the distant mountains, shrouded in gray mist, had grown no closer. A flutter rose in McDonough's stomach. The night would be cold again. The clouds had not moved back in, so there would be no new snow to soften the frozen sheet that lay across the entire valley. The moon, an icy sliver of a thing, lifted into the purpling sky, winking at the westering sun. There were perhaps two hours of daylight left, and no place within sight to find shelter.

An hour later McDonough noticed that the ground was rising. With his forward view shortened, he urged the horses to a quicker pace, anxious to crest the shallow rise. When he did, he found that he was on a low, wide mesa that had a commanding view of the valley surrounding it.

Then he caught a whiff of woodsmoke ... and some-thing else. Bread! Someone was baking bread. The smell of it almost made him swoon from hunger and relief. He saw the thin wisp of chimney smoke against the deep blue sky even before he saw the town. It wasn't much but in that instant it was more welcome than a feather bed.

The town was larger than he expected, stuck out in the middle of nowhere as it was. He was north of the

Yellowstone River, of that he was certain. He hadn't run into the Musselshell River yet so he was somewhere between them on that vast plain of grass and hills and frozen, winter-bare trees. He had gotten himself turned around, and the thought of it made him chuckle to himself. He had spent too many years on his own, traveling from one territory to the next, to get spun around like a kid playing pin the tail. But the snow had come up and played havoc with his inner compass. At least he was still heading west, he mused.

As he got closer he began to make out individual buildings. There were several houses on the outskirts of town, made of stone or clapboard. As he entered the town he saw a few wrought-iron fences wrapped around the small houses, holding in snowdrifts on tiny plots of land. In the spring and summer there would be flowers and vegetables behind those gates, and children playing with cloth balls. Now the yards were frozen and the houses glowed with the warmth of cookstoves and fireplaces.

Further into town he saw a double row of buildings that were mostly constructed of clapboard. They were scoured from the wind and bleached by the sun, gray and cracked. A few of the buildings were in terrible disrepair, leaning this way or that. Others, like the Plains Café at the head of the street, were well-kept, cheerful places, alive with secret activity behind coal-heated incandescence.

McDonough paused outside the café for only a moment. The smell of bread came from here. And fried chicken and steak grilling. He could almost hear the steak sizzle. His stomach tightened and spoke angrily.

Reluctantly he pushed on. First, he had to see to the horses.

A cross-street rolled off the wide mesa to the north-east

and bisected the town, dividing it into quarters. In the next block was a livery stable, its doors shuttered against the cold.

McDonough dismounted and knocked on the small door set inside the larger stable door. He waited impatiently then banged on the door again, and kicked it a few times for good measure.

A latch was thrown from the inside and the door cracked open. A small, gruff face peeked out, squinting.

'Yeah?' A line of tobacco juice sluiced down the man's chin and got absorbed in his scraggly beard.

'Want to board my horses for a few days,' McDonough said, shivering. A musty jet of air had escaped the stable and washed over him. Instead of warming him it sent chills through his body, reminding him just how cold he was.

'Kind of stupid being out in this, ain't it, mister?' The grizzled fellow cackled a little.

'Yeah.'

The man grunted with disappointment. McDonough had not risen to the bait.

Another latch clacked from inside and one of the stable doors opened.

'Close that up fast, mister!'

McDonough hurried the mare and Red through the door. They needed no urging. The scent of hay and the warm air called to them like a siren song. McDonough closed the door, latched it, then turned to look about. It was a fair-sized livery barn with eight stalls, two of them occupied. The grizzled fellow had moved off to the side and was now standing in the doorway to his office. A stove burned behind him and light from two windows cast pale rectangles into the stables. McDonough was standing squarely in the light. He had not removed his found hat

13

and coat, or the woolen scarf that he had wrapped around his face.

The liveryman stood frozen in place, staring hard at the horses. After a moment, his head turned toward McDonough. The man was a silhouette in the light, silent as a ghost.

'How much—' McDonough began.

The liveryman interrupted, tremulously. 'Didn't mean to keep ya waiting out in the cold.'

McDonough shrugged. 'Wouldn't want to open up on a day like this either. How much for the two horses?' He went to the animals and began stripping their saddles and blankets, wiping them down. He found a brush and gave each a good currying.

The grizzled fellow didn't answer right away.

'Jaynes, isn't it?' McDonough asked. He had seen the cracked and peeling sign above the door.

'Yessir,' Jaynes said uncertainly.

'Four bits per day for each horse?' McDonough asked.

'That's just fine.' Jaynes's voice shook. He hadn't moved from the doorway. McDonough waited for Jaynes to take the animals and put them in stalls. Eventually he shrugged and did it himself.

'What's wrong with you?' McDonough could not keep irritation from his voice.

'Nothin'.'

'I want 'em fed good. Oats if you've got 'em.'

'Sure. I got. No problem.'

'And plenty of water. Things've been a mite dry.'

'OK,' Jaynes said, sounding almost breathless now.

Again McDonough paused. Usually when a stranger came to town – especially small towns out in the middle of nowhere – folks were quick to ask questions. News was a

14

commodity out on the prairie. You could trade a home-cooked meal for some, a few drinks for a good story. This Jaynes fellow had no interest in asking questions and clearly wanted McDonough gone.

'Don't forget to close up,' McDonough told the livery-man as he stepped back out into the cold, saddle bags slung over his shoulder. He had left the old Sharps in the gray's saddle boot and took his own Spencer in his mittened fist. The door slammed behind him.

Across the street was a small hotel. Next to that a saloon, one of three in town he had seen. Toward the end of the previous block was the café. Hungry as he was he didn't feel he could go too many more steps. He needed to sit on something wasn't moving, drink some coffee, and let some heat seep back into his bones before he went for food. Saloon, then, he decided, crunching across the snow.

The place was called Danvers' Retreat, and it looked like many of the saloons McDonough had seen over the years. The ceiling was a little higher, perhaps, the room a little wider, the bar a little shorter. But much the same as other whiskey haunts. Evenly spaced about the room were two black stoves that shimmered with heat. Three men were playing cards at a table close to one of the stoves. Another fellow, asleep on his hands, crowded near the other.

Entering, McDonough noticed the bartender do a double-take. He was a long, thin fellow with wild mustaches and long, greasy hair that clung to the sides of his head. He wore a shirt and vest, but it was balmy enough inside to forgo heavier clothing. McDonough sighed as he took off his mittens and unbuttoned the sheepskin coat.

'Could use some coffee,' he said. He was working his

stiff fingers, blowing into them.

The bartender squinted in the dim light and pushed his face across the bar, closer to McDonough.

'Something wrong?'

The bartender shook his head, his face twisted with confusion.

'Ain't got no coffee. Want coffee you go down to the Plains Café. Adele'll fix you up.'

McDonough sighed again, his shoulders slumping.

'Whiskey,' he said, and dropped a coin on the bar. 'I think I'll go sit with my friend over there,' he added, taking the filled glass and his change.

The sleeping man did not wake as McDonough noisily slid the chair out from under the table and spun it around to face the stove. Settling, he loosened his clothing, reveling in the heat that flowed over him.

The card-players had halted their game and cast furtive glances at the newcomer. McDonough smiled beneath his hat brim and lifted his glass in salute before draining it. It burned going down. It had been a while since he had indulged in whiskey.

Remembering the sign outside over the saloon entrance, McDonough lifted his glass and called to the bartender:

' 'Nother one, Danvers.'

The man started at the sound of his name and squinted again. With cautious steps he walked over and poured another measure into McDonough's glass.

'You know me, mister?' Danvers asked in a hushed voice.

'You seem to know me,' McDonough countered.

Danvers shook his head, confused.

'Sure as I think so, but can't hardly be.'

Grinning, McDonough swallowed the whiskey.

'Fella, right now I'll lay claim to being Grover Cleveland himself if'n it'll get me warm!'

The men at the card-table had given up any pretense of continuing with their game. The man with his back to McDonough had turned around in his chair, arm thrown over the back, and was glaring into the dim light at the newcomer. One of his companions reached out and put a restraining hand on his arm.

'Don't, Pete,' he said.

McDonough looked back to Danvers.

'Get them boys a drink, too,' he told the bartender. Danvers shook his head then his whole body shivered.

Pete stood suddenly, kicking back his chair, spinning all the way around.

'I wouldn't drink water with ya, ya scurvy backstabbin' son of a mule!'

Pete's hand wavered just above the butt of a gun holstered at his hip. Slowly, McDonough stood and set the whiskey glass on the table.

'Look, friend,' McDonough said carefully, 'I ain't armed.' With deliberate motions, he pushed open the flaps of his heavy coat. McDonough rarely traveled with guns strapped to his hips because it made for uncomfortable, dangerous riding. His Remington was still in the saddle bags lying innocently on the table next to the Spencer rifle.

'Good,' Pete said, slowly dropping his hand to his gun. 'That'll make things easier.'

CHAPTER TWO

A blackened grin spread across Pete's face. His hand, dropping, picked up speed in a jerking motion toward the heavy black revolver at his side. He crouched slightly as he moved, twisted his shoulder a bit. McDonough had time to marvel at the wasted motions, the amateurish draw, the wild actions prompted by a head and thoughts numbed by too much alcohol.

With a smooth toss of his hand, McDonough swept up the Spencer rifle by the barrel and flicked it like a lariat. The thick hickory stock seemed to snap in the air then slammed into Pete's rising wrist like a three-pound hammer. The sound of bone cracking echoed an instant before Pete's involuntary spasm squeezed off a wasted bullet, splintering the floor at the gunman's feet. Pete screamed and his revolver dropped to the floor with a thud.

Crying with rage, Pete fell to his knees and tried to scoop up the gun as he held his useless wrist.

'Don't, friend,' McDonough said. He had flipped the Spencer over in a blurring motion so that the gaping barrel mouth now stared down at Pete, barely three inches from the man's nose. 'I wouldn't want you to get the wrong idea about me, but I'll kill you if you reach for that hogleg.'

He said it with a pleasant smile on his face, and tossed his gaze at Pete's friends, all too stunned to move. McDonough looked over at Danvers. The bartender had taken several steps backwards toward the bar.

'Danvers, my old pal,' McDonough said sarcastically, 'you don't want to be grabbing up any Greener might be behind that bar.'

Danvers froze in mid-step and shook his head.

'You'd better get on out of here, mister. Whoever you are,' Danvers told him, squinting desperately.

McDonough laughed. 'And here I thought we was old bosom buddies.'

The motionless friends now came alive. Neither of them reached for his gun, but they turned toward Danvers rumbling with a mix of confusion and anger.

'You half-blind idjit! You know this feller!' they insisted.

Danvers shook his head. 'No, I don't. An' neither do you fellas. Now git, mister. And don't come back.'

Cradling the rifle in his armpit, McDonough buttoned his borrowed coat and adjusted his hat. Then he grabbed up the saddle bags and backed toward the door. Pete was still on the floor, whimpering, breathing huskily, and babying his broken wrist.

'You best get that looked after, friend,' McDonough said. 'I done you a favor, breaking that wrist of yours. One day you were bound to draw on the wrong fella and get yourself killed.'

'I ain'ta done with you, you sidewinder.' Pete spat the words but made no motion to back them up with gunplay.

Outside in the blustering cold again, McDonough sighed. What had happened made no sense and that angered him. All he wanted was to get warm and have a meal and sleep in a bed for a night before pushing on.

Then some hot-headed rummy decided to pick a fight. Fools. No wonder he stayed away from towns. Well, he'd go eat, then sleep, and tomorrow, after he'd found Clara, he'd light a shuck and be shed of this town.

Glancing over at the livery stable he saw that the light was out in the office. The place looked empty. Now that he thought of it, that liveryman had acted strangely, too, much as Danvers and Pete had reacted. Afraid, nervous. Like they had seen a ghost.

Looking himself over – at the found hat and sheepskin coat – he suddenly realized why. They had mistaken him for someone else. The dead man, no doubt. Both the stable and the saloon had been dark. Too dark to make out facial features. But light enough to see the hat and the coat.

'Blast it,' he muttered aloud. 'What have I stepped into?'

He had been in the saloon longer than he had thought. The sun was dipping down toward a misty horizon. The whiskey had warmed him, but not enough to sustain him for long. Already he was feeling the press of frigid air. Behind him was a hotel, but he figured they'd take his money any time. He was hungry. The smells coming from the café were too inviting to be ignored. Steeling himself against the blustery wind, he put his head down and walked to the end of the boardwalk then stepped down into the snow-crusted street. The reddish glow coming from the cafe's distant windows beckoned to him.

He met no one on the street, though he did see a few curious faces peering out of darkened storefronts. Ignoring them he slogged on toward the café. He was a few yards from the front door when he heard the thunder of approaching horses.

'There he is!' someone cried out.

Whirling to face them, McDonough dropped his saddle bags and brought the Spencer up to his shoulder. There were six of them atop smoking horses, three of them had guns drawn.

The speaker pointed with his gun.

'I've got him, Mr Forester,' he said. He was cocking the revolver when McDonough sent a shot smashing into the man's shoulder.

The other two fired wildly, their horses spooked by the echoing boom of McDonough's Spencer. Turned around, the riders tried to reach back and throw more lead.

'Stop it, you fools,' a thick-chested, white-bearded man bellowed.

The three unarmed men jumped out of their saddles and rushed McDonough, who was reluctant to fire on them. They swarmed over him, slapping at him, throwing punches at his body. His borrowed coat took most of the punishment.

McDonough kicked out with a boot and caught one man in the groin. Stepping around the fallen man he swung a heavy fist into the jaw of another, dropping him. The third one took a step back and settled himself, squared his shoulders. He brought thick hands up toward his face and balled them into fists, affecting a fighter's stance. The knuckles of each hand were scraped and bruised. He was close to six feet, with a tight jaw and thin lips. His eyes were too close together, giving him an evil look. It was sure that this man loved to fight.

With an audible sigh, McDonough raised his own fists, shed of their mittens, and waited. The fighter stepped forward and threw a fast left-right-left combination. McDonough dodged the first two and deflected the third, then sent a surprise left jab into the man's nose. Blood shot out in two quick streams. The fighter barely flinched.

'Gibson! Stop it!' The command brought instant still-ness. The fighter, Strap Gibson, lowered his fists, but continued to glare at McDonough's dark face, partly hidden by the sombrero.

McDonough glanced up at the only man still atop his horse. It was the older, bearded fellow. Forester, someone had called him.

'He's not Gregory,' Forester said, derisively. 'Any idiot could tell that.'

Gibson straightened and tightened his stare. In that moment all his muscles seemed to relax at once.

Behind Forester the others were holstering their weapons. The man McDonough had shot was helped to his feet. A blotch of red discolored his coat at the shoul-der. Beyond them McDonough could see the liveryman, Forester's informant, leading his horse, trying to sneak back into the stables.

'You always treat strangers this way?' McDonough asked angrily.

'How'd you get that coat? That hat?' Forester demanded in return.

A quick sneer twisted McDonough's face.

'To the devil with you. All of you.'

Gibson stiffened and took a step forward.

'Mr Forester asked you a question.'

McDonough bent over and picked up his fallen rifle and saddle bags, keeping one eye on the cantankerous Strap Gibson. The others had calmed by now – all, that was, except the wounded man – and none of them was keen on continuing the fight.

'I'm hungry and I'm cold and I just finished a fight with another hothead. I don't want any more trouble,'

McDonough told them. 'If you need to talk to me, you'll come inside and watch me eat.'

'No,' Forester said slowly. 'I don't care who you are.'

The older man pulled hard on the reins, turning his large stallion. He was careless in his movements and knocked into two of his own men.

'Wait a minute!' McDonough called out. 'Answer me something. Where can I find Clara?'

Forester paused and twisted in the saddle. 'Who?'

'Clara.'

'Don't know anyone by that name.'

McDonough nodded and, without another word, entered the café.

The air within the restaurant was thick with humidity and cooking smells. The contrast from the dry, cold weather outside made McDonough pause, struggling for breath. Lanterns gave a bright yellow glaze to the place. Tables dotted the room here and there, disarrayed from earlier meals. Two diners sat at one table sipping coffee, cowhands lingering in the warmth before heading back outside. A pot-bellied stove shimmered with heat in the middle of the room.

There were clanking sounds through a swinging door back of the short lunch counter. The counter was low with an odd assortment of chairs pushed up to it in haphazard fashion. There was a small order window and shelf at the back of the room close to the swinging door that led to the kitchen. Through it, McDonough saw some quick move-ments, heard metal scrapping sounds, but nothing distin-guishable. A strange chatter drifted out of that window. It took a moment for him to recognize the staccato sounds of Chinese.

'*Wui naam! Wui naam!*' a woman said, pausing in the doorway, looking back into the kitchen.

She was answered by a high-pitched, shrill voice, then waved her hand in a dismissive gesture and stepped fully into the room. She stopped sharply when she saw McDonough.

'Ma'am,' he said, noting the momentary surprise in her large round eyes.

Her face pinched slightly, then she huffed with a silent chuckle.

'Sit anywhere, stranger.'

McDonough looked the room over again and chose a table close to the kitchen. She followed him, placing silverware and a checkered napkin on the bare wood table. She glanced only briefly at the Spencer rifle he placed in a handy corner and at the thickly packed saddle bags he dropped onto a vacant chair.

She paused looking down at him, waiting. With a self-conscious gesture, McDonough swept the sombrero from his head and dropped it onto the saddle bags. An odd flutter of relief passed over the woman's face.

'We've got better tables than this,' she told him.

He tossed a glance over at the large windows at the front of the café.

'Wanted to stay away from them.'

'Sure,' she said, scowling. 'I saw the ruckus. Look, if there's going to be trouble I'd just as soon see you leave.'

McDonough laughed. 'No, ma'am, I just can't go out into that cold right now. Trouble's all over anyway. Besides, I sat here for the warmth. It's a mite chilly close to that glass.'

She looked over at the windows and nodded.

'What'll it be?'

24

'What've ya got?' he asked, grinning.

She ran down a short menu of fried chicken, steak, beef-stew, eggs, and canned green beans.

'You got good steaks?'

'Mister, this is cow country. Steaks we've got a-plenty, and they're good enough for you.'

'Well, then I'll have me two of them and any greens you might have. Oh, and I smelled bread coming into town.'

'That was mine.' Her shoulders squared a little with pride.

'I'll take a hunk of that, too.'

She hadn't written down anything, just stood over him, watching with arms crossed and an almost defiant flame in her eyes.

'I figure you might could use some coffee, too,' she added. 'Smells like you've had a snootful.'

'Snootful!' McDonough said, slapping his knee. 'Why, ma'am, two shots of whiskey might pass for a good drunk in this part of the country, but where I'm from babies don't get pie-eyed on that little drink.'

A crooked smile began working its way across her mouth.

'Fact is,' he added, 'I went into that saloon looking for coffee.'

'A saloon for coffee, huh?'

'God's honest truth. I was just plumb frozen. I didn't figure I could make it down to this end of town without something to warm me.'

Her smile hadn't quite finished before it ran out of steam. But it didn't fade away entirely and McDonough figured that that was the best he would get from her.

'I'll get your food,' she told him, and went to the kitchen. A moment later she came back with a bowl

25

heaped with fat slices of bread. 'Your steaks'll be up in a few minutes.'

The bread was still warm and soft and McDonough took no time devouring three slices. After, he settled back and loosened his coat and scarf. For brief moments he could see the woman at work through the order window. She was a handsome woman, he decided. Not really beautiful, but attractive. Hers was a face he wouldn't forget. It was long and square. She had an aquiline nose that ended with a small bulb well above a modest, round mouth. Her eyes were a yellowish-green color and large. Her forehead was high. She wore a long mass of umber hair bound in green ribbon and thrown over one shoulder. Watching her go from the dining-room to the kitchen and back again, he saw that she had a trim, almost athletic figure hidden beneath the long, plain skirt and the unadorned white blouse she wore. His appreciative gaze never left her as she brought his order to the table.

McDonough wasted no time slicing off a juicy piece of the thick steak and shoving it into his mouth.

'Well,' he mumbled through the food, 'you don't lie!'

'No. I don't.'

'Ma'am, you probably've watched more people eat than you care to,' he said, swallowing, 'but I've been on the trail for three weeks and haven't spoke to a soul but my horse in all that time. I could do with a bit of conversation.'

'The dinner crowd'll be coming in soon.' The excuse sounded hollow even to her ears.

' 'Til they do?'

She nodded, turned away to the counter, and picked up an empty coffee cup. Sitting down next to him, she poured coffee into her cup and some more into his. His mouth filled again, he just smiled.

'Danvers at the saloon said you're Adele.'

'Adele Chappell.'

McDonough put down his knife and fork, stuck out his hand and introduced himself. She huffed another silent chuckle, a smile growing on her lips. She took his hand and shook it firmly.

'Where do you hail from, Mr McDonough?'

'All over, ma'am,' he said, his mouth full again. 'But I was last in South Dakota. Working my way to Oregon, or so I thought.' He told her about the sudden snowstorm and getting turned around in it. 'Fact is, I ain't got a clue as to where I am.'

This brought a full-throated laugh from Adele which McDonough found infectious. He laughed through a mouthful of steak.

'You are in Sprigensguth, a small dot in Montana Territory. You're smack dab in the middle of cow country. We've got us a few big outfits and a dozen or more smaller ranches. Sprigensguth serves them all.'

'Big outfits, huh? Think I mighta run into one of them.'

Adele grinned. 'You did. That was Alexander Forester. He's been here since God put grass on the hillside.'

'Grass,' McDonough snorted. 'I ain't seen a blade of it since I got into the territory.'

'Well, if you're around this spring you'll see plenty of it. Green as far as the eye can see.' She nodded out the window, her eyes flitting to a spot at the end of the street. 'There's an outcropping of rock at the edge of the mesa. I sometimes go there in the spring and climb to the top of it. You can see everything from there. The valley is filled end to end with cattle.'

'Got a glimpse of it on the way in. That's a lot of cows.'

Adele smiled. 'I suppose you'll want to hook up with an

outfit. You sure aren't going to make it across the Bitterroot Range in winter.'

McDonough nodded glumly. 'Darn fool I was. Got a late start and lost my way. Good cooking does it to me every time.'

'I'll bet it was the pies she baked that kept you around,' Adele said in a mildly teasing way.

'Nope. Was a fella named Tulesko. He had a small outfit and did his own cookin' for the boys. Heard tell he had been a chef back in Ohio before getting the itch to travel. The man could make bacon and beans dance on your tongue.'

Adele watched his eyes flare with enthusiasm as he talked of food. She couldn't help smiling at him. Both of his steaks were gone, the green beans had vanished minutes ago, and the last slab of bread was in the process of being devoured. She got up and went to the kitchen, disappearing only a moment before returning with a thick slice of dried apple pie.

'Here,' she said. 'On the house.'

His grin widened to take in most of his face, and his eyes danced with a joyful light.

'Why, thank you, ma'am!'

Sitting again she said: 'There might be a couple of outfits still looking for a winter hand, but I wouldn't get my hopes up.'

He shrugged. 'Whatever's handy. I ain't afraid of work. Just need me a place to hold up 'til this blue norther blows over.'

'Blue norther!' Adele laughed. 'Why, where you come from this might be considered cold but in weather like this we here still go down to the swimming-hole of Saturday afternoon for a dip.'

McDonough slapped his knee hard and hurrahed wildly, covering his mouth so not to spray pie all over Adele. The Chinese cook peeked up over the order window then, mumbling, ducked his head back out of sight.

'I deserved that one,' he said. 'I surely did.'

They sat for a moment, quietly enjoying the company. McDonough eventually pushed the empty pie-plate away and settled back in his chair and patted his stomach.

'What's in Oregon?' she asked.

'Beats me. But I aim to see it.'

'Well, I can make you a list of ranchers to talk, if you like. You can go calling on them tomorrow. Now, I have to get ready for the supper crowd. Is there anything else I can get you?'

McDonough thought a moment then asked:

'You wouldn't happen to have an envelope would you?'

'I – I don't think so,' she told him.

'Got me a letter to write. Which, by the way, I wanted to ask you. Do you know a gal name of Clara?'

She shook her head. 'Can't say I do. As for the envelope you might try over at the general store at the end of the block.'

'I will. And, ma'am, thank you for the conversation.'

Smiling, she said. 'You're welcome. But call me Adele.'

'I will, Adele. I'm Rafe. And who knows, when the thaw comes I might just find I like this here territory just fine.'

'Not you, cowboy,' she said, shaking her head. Her eyes were lit with a smile. 'You've got wanderer written all over you.'

McDonough nodded. 'That's true. It can be lonesome, though, that wandering.'

'Yes,' she agreed, a wistful smile on her lips, 'it surely can be that.'

Adele cleared the table. McDonough readied himself to leave, bundling tightly and shoving the black sombrero onto his head. Adele came back into the dining room and stopped short. For just a heartbeat she was startled by the wrapped figure in front of her. McDonough saw her eyes widen for that split second.

'I don't suppose you want to tell me about it, Adele. I've been getting looks like the one on your face since I got to town.'

A conflict of emotions played out in her eyes. At last she shook her head.

'OK.' McDonough dropped some coins on the table. 'I'll come for that list tomorrow. Good night.'

She called to him when he reached the door. 'Rafe. You might want to get another hat before you go visiting ranches tomorrow.'

A wry smile grew across his lips. He reached up and touched the wide, flat brim of the sombrero. His fingers fell on a brittle spot. Even without seeing it he knew it was a patch of dried blood.

'I'll do that,' he said. 'By the way, have you folks got a sheriff in this town?'

She didn't even try to hide her surprise. 'Why?'

'Might like to pass the time of day with him. You got one?'

'We've a constable. He's around.'

McDonough tipped his hat and pushed out of the café.

CHAPTER THREE

The owner of the general store had no envelopes. He had no voice, either, apparently. His eyes widened as soon as McDonough stepped into the store. As he removed the sombrero, McDonough revealed a pleasant smile and amused dark eyes in an attempt to allay the man's fear. But when asked about envelopes the store-owner, a cadaverous old coot, shook his head vigorously, stepping behind a protective counter. McDonough hadn't expected to find what he needed. He wasn't even certain he needed an envelope. He had thought to write a letter to the dead man's woman, Clara, with news of his passing. But so far no one had even heard of her. Or if they had, they weren't telling.

On his way out the door he spotted a shelf full of hats and detoured over to them. For the most part they were of good quality, sturdy, warm. McDonough hesitated over them, his fingers twiddling on a brim or a crown. No, he decided, he'd keep the sombrero. At least for now. There was something about it that stirred up this town and until he could find his answers that was the way he wanted things.

McDonough was no rough rider. He kept the motto of live and let live. Traveling as he did, he didn't have occasion to make enemies. If things got difficult he would pull

31

up stakes and leave. It was a good life, he had reflected more than once. He was beholden to no man, lived in the open air, worked when he needed, and had seen much of the country west of the Mississippi. True, he had no home other than Red and the saddle. But neither did he have any of the complications a sedentary life brought to bear.

Yet this man's death had disturbed him. Lying alone, frozen, half-covered in snow and blood, the man had appeared so fragile. He had died alone, and had taken some time in doing it. He had bled to death, slowly freezing, trapped in a body that wouldn't respond, his mind probably active, more alert than it had ever been. McDonough shivered at the image. He wondered what the man's last thoughts had been. Whether they had been of his killer or of the woman named Clara.

Regardless, the man had died alone. And apparently hated, if the reaction in town was any indication. Well, being hated didn't excuse murder. McDonough wanted to find Clara, needed to find her. The man might have died alone, but McDonough would see to it that he was remembered well by at least one person.

The hotel had a room for him on the second floor, a small but serviceable place with a soft bed. He was brought several blankets, clean, threadbare sheets, a hot-water bottle, and some glowing coals for the stove set off in one corner of the room. While not balmy, the room quickly became comfortable. Without realizing it, he drifted off to sleep.

McDonough was used to the trail, often rising before the sun. He did so the next morning but allowed himself to drift back to sleep. When he next opened his eyes, the sun was full up and shining its white-yellow light into the room. Staring out the window at the snow-covered mesa he dressed in the woolen pants, plaid shirt, and suspenders he had been wearing for days. With the Crazy Mountains behind him, his view was of an endlessly bleak tract of frozen, gently rolling land.

Something caught his eye out the window and he craned his neck to see it better. There was an outcropping of rock, coated now with ice and snow, at the end of the mesa. He felt a smile rise to his lips as he remembered Adele's story. This was her top of the world.

He tried to heat some water on the stove but the coals were dying. He washed hurriedly, shivering, and chose not to shave. Amused by his own reflection in the shaving-mirror, he rubbed his ruddy face. In his heart he was still young, but his youth had been lost somewhere on his back-trail. What looked back at him was a man of thirty who, weathered as he was, could have been forty. He was a scraggy looking fellow, he decided with a chuckle. His mass of grayish-yellow hair had a hint of red in it, and his beard matched. His eyes were dark, almost black, but they had a bright sheen that gave them a friendly appearance. His face was oval, mouth maybe a little too wide, at least for his liking. He stood six feet in stockings and was built lean. His right hip rode slightly higher than the left. It was something others couldn't see, but it was the reason he didn't wear a gun all the time. Guns were not a comfortable fit for him.

Despite the large supper he had eaten the night before he felt his stomach rumble with hunger. He took the coal pan out of the stove and brought it down to the bleary-eyed clerk.

'I'll be needing the room another few days, if that's all right.'

The clerk dumped the coal into a larger stove in the back office.

'We'll manage to squeeze you in, mister,' he called back

sarcastically. 'Not many holiday travelers this time of year.'

'Say, can I ask you something?'

The clerk stepped back to the counter adjusting his wire-rimmed glasses.

'Sure.'

'Do you recognize this hat?'

Studying the sombrero on McDonough's head, the clerk shook his head.

'It's one of them Texican sombreros, ain't it?'

McDonough nodded. 'Something like that.'

'Never seen it afore. Looks kinda smudged. I could get it cleaned for you, if you like.'

'No. It's fine the way it is. Thanks.'

The day was bright and clear and warmer than the day before, although his breath still puffed around his mouth. The freezing wind had died.

The hotel was on the town's lone cross-street. McDonough left, and walked to the intersection, across the main street and to the end of the road where a small stone-and-wood jail stood. Unadorned with porch or windows, the building looked lonely in its isolation. A hand-painted sign swung from a wooden arm and read:

JAIL
Constable Thackery.

McDonough used the rough-hewn logs in front of the door to step up into the jail.

'You the law around here?' he asked, closing the door behind him.

At the desk sat a youngish man, Constable Thackery. Like most of the people in this town he was lean and looked rubbed raw by the elements. He wore a trimmed beard,

34

black as the thick patch of hair on his wide head. Thackery was alone. The two cells behind him sat empty and their doors were cracked open. There were two more chairs in the room, a board with dodgers pinned to it, a tiny file cabinet, a stove fighting to keep out the cold, and a gun rack.

Thackery stood and thrust out a hand.

'Nels Thackery,' he said. 'I'm what passes for law around here.'

'Rafe McDonough, last out of the Dakotas.'

'Not your home, then?'

'I wander.'

Thackery had stepped around the desk and gone to the stove. He picked up the coffee-pot warming there. He poured two mugs full and handed one to McDonough.

'And your wandering brings you here.'

Thackery had tried to keep his voice and his actions casual, but his eyes betrayed him. They were drawn in furtive glances up to the black sombrero. McDonough explained about his travels and his need for work.

'You might hook on with a ranch hereabouts,' Thackery said. 'Not much other work in town unless one of the saloons is looking to hire.'

McDonough cocked his head. 'Ain't much use indoors, Constable.'

Thackery grinned as he sipped his coffee. 'No. You belong out on the range.' They drank silently, eyeing one another, then Thackery asked: 'What brings you to my door?'

McDonough took off the hat and tossed it onto the desk.

'You know who wears a hat like this?'

Thackery ignored the sombrero and looked up at McDonough.

'I might.'

'Good-sized fella, good-looking, too. Wears a gun tied down.'

Thackery nodded.

'He's dead. On my backtrail, somewhere.'

'You kill him?'

'No. He'd been dead a while before I stumbled onto him.'

'You can't say where he is?'

McDonough shook his head. 'Got turned around like a greenhorn. Figure it wasn't more than half a day's ride in good weather.' He explained how he had found the body, and that he had taken the clothing for warmth.

'Four shots,' Thackery shrugged. 'That'll kill a man.'

'I think maybe he bled to death, or froze when the storm moved in. There was a lot of blood under the body and the bullet holes were small.'

'Well, he'll keep 'til spring. Somebody'll find him.'

McDonough's face tightened. 'You don't seem all that concerned. And you say you know the man?'

'Of him. Sounds like Dick Gregory. He used to be one of Alex Forester's hands, but he got fired, run off the range.'

'Not before he got a beating,' McDonough said, anger creeping into his voice.

'If you're thinking Forester killed him you're just plumb wrong. Forester's too big. He doesn't need to kill to get what he wants.'

'Nobody needs to kill. It's a choice he makes.'

'Maybe. But it's never been Forester's choice.'

McDonough put his cup down and turned for the door.

'Thank you, Constable. Oh, by the way, I'm looking for a woman named Clara. Don't have a last name.'

Thackery's face came alive now with curiosity.

'No,' he said. McDonough sensed the man was telling the truth. 'I've not heard of a Clara in these parts. Why?'

'Someone a friend asked me to look up. Thanks anyway.'

The black sombrero fitted snugly again to his head, McDonough walked back into the center of town and turned toward the café. He moved slowly, feeling uneasy. He didn't know yet if he liked Thackery; didn't know if the man was lazy or tightlipped or simply in Forester's pocket. He paused and looked down the street. It was empty and quiet, yet he could feel eyes on him. He wondered, not for the first time, if it was worth the trouble to keep looking for something no one seemed to want found. But he kept coming back to a simple fact. A man was dead and the one person he had cared for should be told. It was clear that Constable Thackery wouldn't be doing that job.

At the end of the street breakfast and the Plains Café beckoned. Maybe this Dick Gregory fellow hadn't been from around here, McDonough thought. If Clara lived somewhere else all together he wouldn't find her by hanging around Sprigensguth. He was headed toward Oregon, but there was nothing waiting for him there. He could ride south just as easily. There would be other towns in which he could find work, places where the sight of a black sombrero and a heavy sheepskin coat didn't stir men to violence.

Still, if this town knew Gregory enough to hate him so fiercely there might be someone in it who had heard the name Clara. He owed no duty to the dead man, although he felt he did. It was an irrational emotion, he knew, but a powerful one.

He had just stepped into the street when his hat was suddenly yanked from his head, flying off behind him. He whirled to find a woman studying the sombrero, with one eyebrow prettily cocked on her high forehead. She wasn't tall, maybe five-four. Under a heavy coat it was difficult to tell her much about her figure. She wore a man's hat with

37

a short brim and the crown creased, the brim curled up along the back. Her hair was a golden-brown color, long and straight in a peek-a-boo sweep over part of her face. Her blue eyes, slim nose, and full mouth fitted perfectly inside an almost dainty oval face. The cold added a blush to her cheeks.

'You've got to get you a better hat, stranger,' she said. Her voice was rich, a little husky, very inviting.

'So I've been told.'

'Everybody in town would like to put a bullet right through that sombrero.'

McDonough took back his hat and slipped it onto his head.

'Including you?'

'Mm-mm,' she said, shaking her head. 'I don't shoot my problems away. My name is Helen Cormier, I run the Box-J. I'd like to talk to you.'

'Can we do it somewhere warmer?' he suggested.

'I'll do better'n that. I'll buy you breakfast.' Helen slipped her arm through his and guided him down the street.

Once inside the café Helen doffed her thick coat to reveal a trim figure in brown corduroy pants tucked into calf-high boots, suspenders, and a blue shirt. Man's clothing that fitted to her form in a tantalizing way.

A few eyes turned toward them as they entered, then turned away again. Helen pointed to a table and they sat. She smiled brightly as Adele came up to them.

' 'Morning, Adele. Looks like the storm didn't keep everyone away.'

'We're usually busier than this, Helen. I'm surprised to see you in town so early.' Adele's face was strained, with a tightness in her voice that McDonough picked up on instantly. 'Glad to see you're back, Rafe.'

'Well, I told you good cookin' does it for me every time.'

'Yes,' Helen said, 'Adele runs a nice restaurant.'

'Thank you.'

They gave their order. Helen waited for Adele to leave before speaking. She fingered the sombrero again, thrown hastily onto a chair by McDonough as he sat.

'I meant what I said about getting a new hat.'

'You know who this belongs to?'

'Looks like the one Dick Gregory wears. He worked for me for a spell. Things didn't work out.'

'Know him well?'

'Not really. Didn't talk much. Where did you meet him?'

She held his eyes firmly, a pleasant smile on her face, waiting.

'On the trail out of town,' he told her, feeling a twinge in his stomach. He hadn't wanted to lie, and he hadn't, really. But after meeting with the constable he had decided to be cautious with everything concerning Dick Gregory.

'Well, you sure caused a stir hereabouts. I heard that Forester himself raced in and sicced some of his men on you.' She was nearly laughing saying it. 'Word gets around quickly in a small town like this.'

'What did he have against Gregory?'

'Not much. Enough to have his chief bulldog, Strap Gibson, beat the man half to death. Forester found out Gregory was doing a little night expressing with the cattle he was supposed to be watching.'

'That's a hanging offense where I come from.' He smiled up at Adele as she returned and set plates of food before them.

'Forester isn't that sort,' Helen said.

'So I hear.'

They talked while they ate, McDonough explaining his circumstances, where he had worked and for whom. Through her father, Helen said she knew of Tulesko and another of the ranchers for whom McDonough had worked. Adele filled their coffee mugs several times.

'Heard you were looking for work. That's one of the reasons I came in to town so early. Wanted to catch you before you left. I could use a man at my spread.'

'Well, I'm looking for a place to light this winter.'

'Maybe,' she said, looking past the sweep of hair that fell over one eye, 'you'll like it well enough to stay more than the winter.'

'Maybe.'

She nodded. 'I've got a spread south of here. It'll be slow going with the snow, but we can make it back there before nightfall. If you'll take the job.'

'I need to check out of the hotel and get my horses.'

'That's fine. My horse is at the livery barn as well, but I've got to put in an order at the general store first. I can meet you at the horses.'

Adele came over and took money and compliments from Helen. The restaurant-owner smiled at McDonough.

'Guess this is goodbye for a while,' Adele said.

'I reckon so. I'm not one to come into town of a Saturday night for gambling and whiskey.'

'You could come in for a meal.'

'I could at that.'

'He'll be back soon enough, Adele,' Helen told her. 'I need a man to come in and get some supplies.'

'You still have Sven, don't you?' The fire that McDonough had seen in Adele's eyes last night flared again. There was more than a bit of mischief in the woman, he thought, holding back a grin.

'Some things boys just aren't equipped to handle,' Helen said sweetly.

'I wouldn't know. I've never bothered with boys.'

For just the briefest instant Helen stiffened. She nodded her goodbyes, then with a measured gait strode from the room. Outside, she stopped on the street and turned to McDonough. She seemed about to say something, paused, then continued across to the general store.

'I was serious about that hat,' she told him. 'Come into the store with me and I'll buy you a new one.'

'Thanks. But I think I'll keep this one just the same. For now.'

Helen looked at him through narrowed eyes.

'It's your business if you want to wear a target,' she said matter-of-factly. 'I'll meet you at the livery barn.'

After settling his bill and retrieving his belongings at the hotel, McDonough roused the bleary-eyed old stable hand and settled with him. The man was still jittery at the sight of McDonough and he kept his eyes averted from the sombrero. With both horses saddled, McDonough turned from the barn to wait in the street. Helen was only minutes behind him. Silently she readied her own horse then rode out at a quick gait. McDonough spurred Red forward to follow, pulling the mare behind him.

They rode in silence for half an hour, angling down off the mesa. Helen had taken them past the café but resisted the urge to turn and look in. McDonough had seen her struggle with that decision and held a grin from popping up on his face. There was some bad blood between those two, he thought with amusement.

The day had stayed bright without a cloud to be seen. The sky was deep and so blue the color was almost purple.

While the sun was weak, it did offer some warmth, especially since there was no wind to snatch it away.

Helen's sudden voice startled McDonough.

'What is it you're after, Mr McDonough?' He turned to her in surprise. 'In life, I mean. What is it you want?'

'I'm easy to please, ma'am. A warm place to set my bones. A bit of work. That's all I need.'

'And good cooking, isn't that what you said?'

'After weeks on the trail good cookin' is better'n a soft bed.'

She thought a moment then said: 'Adele was certainly attentive during breakfast. Don't recall her ever filling a coffee-cup so many times. I sure got my money's worth.'

'She seems a fine woman,' he told her, his voice more brittle than he had intended.

'I'm sure she seems that way.'

Silence fell over them for a time. At first McDonough thought they would follow the trail he had taken into town but Helen veered further south toward wooded hills that stood out in sharp relief against the sky and the bright, white ground. He knew those hills to be distant but in the clear air they appeared close enough to touch.

'My range is near those hills,' she told him. 'We'll cross a frozen creek in a bit and that'll be the start of it. I neighbor Forester's land. He's west of me.'

They came upon a few cows, scattered here and there, wandering forlornly, it seemed to McDonough. There wasn't a blade of grass to be seen anywhere. He moved to guide the animals into a bunch. Each wore the Box-J brand.

'Leave them,' Helen said. 'I'll send Sven back to round 'em up.'

Just after midday they crested a low hill. Below in the distance were several low buildings and a herd of about

500 cows bunched tightly around a series of corrals. A few miles beyond were the wooded hills that had hung before them the entire trip. Helen paused and looked down at the ranch with pride.

'The Box-J,' she said.

'Looks mighty comfortable.'

She turned in the saddle.

'It is, Rafe,' she said. 'It's very comfortable. My dad saw to that, and I'm trying to keep it up the way he would have.'

'He's passed, then.'

'Three years ago. It's been hard, Rafe. Very hard. Men don't like dealing with a woman in this business. They think I'm all frills and tears and tea. Well, I've never cried dealing cattle, but I near brought a man to his knees once. I don't care for frills or tea. This is my home, my land, and my cows. I'm making a go of it, but . . . it's hard, Rafe.'

'There are good men to be hired, if you need the help.'

She flared with instant anger. 'I told you, I don't need a man to run things.'

'Even Forester has men working for him. That's all I meant.'

Her eyes widened, then she laughed hoarsely.

'You're right, of course. Forgive me. I just haven't had a lot of luck finding the right man. I've hired a bunch of them. None of them worked out.'

'Like Gregory?'

She shrugged. 'Every one was different. Well, different in some things. They were all alike in one way, though,' she said, coldly. 'Every one of them wanted two things: the land and me. Neither of which has ever been for sale.' She took a long, slow breath. 'My dad left this to me because he knew I could manage it. I won't let him down.'

'I'll do what I can for you, Miss Cormier. At least through the winter.'

'I know you will, Rafe.' She smiled now, and it was like a blast of warm air. 'Just do your job and you'll find I can be a right friendly gal. Oh, Rafe,' she said with a gust of laughter, 'unfurrow that brow of yours, will you? I mean friendly like a man would say it. Do you think me that scheming of a woman?'

'I reckon not.'

'That's better. Now let's get in under cover already. I'm like to freeze out here.'

It took them better than half an hour to ride down to the ranch. Leading the way, Helen pushed through the sea of black and brown cowhide to a latched gate that she unhitched and swung open from the saddle. McDonough followed her in, stepping the horses aside so she could close the gate.

The main house was at the far end of the compound. It was small and squat but looked comfortable with a short porch and stone steps leading up to the front door. Attached at one end was the cookhouse, an overlarge building from which emanated several inviting smells. A few yards away from the cookhouse was the bunkhouse. It was in good repair, a solid-looking building that would probably house six men. A chicken-coop and an iced-over garden lay on the other side of the house. On the opposite side of the compound was a large barn connecting to a stable with a series of corrals leading from them like a spider's web. There were two branding-chutes.

Old-fashioned tepee-shaped bundles of hay had been left out in the corrals and along the outside of the fence for the cows to feed on.

'We rotate the stock in to feed,' she told him. 'It keeps

them from wandering too far off. Most of them, that is.'

Nodding toward the open barn door and the stacks of hay lying within he said:

'Looks like you've enough feed for the winter.'

'This land is a blessing, Rafe. The valley is filled with miles and miles of good grass. It's a job of work cutting it and hauling it back and curing it, but there's plenty of it. The big problem in winter is water. We're out at all hours cracking the ice on these troughs, and on the nearby streams.'

She pointed to a series of troughs, all of them with a thin coating of ice on top.

'Come on, let's warm up and get something to eat. Sven!' she called.

They dismounted, McDonough taking his fat saddle bags and the Spencer rifle. After a moment a tall youth looked out of the barn. Recognizing Helen, he hurried forward.

'Sven,' she said, 'I've brought back another hand. Could you put the horses up and then join us in the cook-house?'

'Sure t'ing, Miss Helen,' he said, beaming broadly.

McDonough rounded his horses, lifted the reins for the boy to take and stopped short when he heard a gasp. Sven was staring at the gray mare and its brand. His head whipped around, eyes glaring at McDonough's sombrero and coat.

'*Avkomma tik!*' he bellowed as he drove a corded fist into McDonough's jaw. 'I told you to stay away or I'd kill you!'

CHAPTER FOUR

His head snapping back, McDonough took the punch flat-footed, unbalanced. He stumbled back against Red's shoulder then rolled as the horse angrily sidestepped. The gray mare whinnied with fright and began tossing its head.

On his knees, McDonough shook his own head, trying to clear it of the sudden buzzing from within. Something hard slammed into his chest. He gasped, hearing a snap and feeling searing pain.

Something was screeching, and he couldn't tell if it was Helen, the horses, or Sven. A boot appeared before him but he managed to turn just before it connected. Rolling, he slapped at the boot, making a grab for its snow-slicked surface.

A body fell. Sven's. But he was on the far side of the mare. More screaming. Too many legs. Then he saw Sven standing over him, the boy's fists balled and shaking.

'Stop!' Helen cried out of the chaos. 'Sven, stop!'

The boy held his ground, unwilling to yield but obeying Helen's command. McDonough looked up to see his face red and full of hate. Then, as if a veil had been removed, Sven blanched. His eyes and his mouth popped open in recognition of what he had done. There were tears in his eyes now and McDonough had the urge to laugh, but didn't for fear of being hit again.

'I'm sorry,' Sven said, reaching down with one of his large, iron-hard paws.

McDonough hesitated only a moment before allowing the youth to help him back to his feet. He winced lightly at the pain in his ribs. He took a long slow breath, waiting for more pain, but none came.

'I thought . . .' the boy stammered.

'Yeah,' McDonough told him. 'I know what you thought.'

Helen was by his side, her mouth twisted a little trying to fight back a smile. She held his sombrero, which had fallen off in the ruckus.

'Told you to get a new hat,' she said. McDonough took the sombrero, brushed snow from its brim, then slid it back onto his head. 'Sven . . . the horses.'

'Oh, ya, Miss Helen. Right away.'

The boy looked shorter now. Contrition had shrunk him a little. He took the three horses by their reins and guided them into the barn. Helen cocked her head toward the cookhouse, motioning for McDonough to follow.

Upon entering the building, McDonough saw a long dining table with bench-seats on opposite sides. A lone wooden armchair sat at one end. Behind and to the left of the table was a doublewide cookstove and two small work tables. At the far end of the room stood a small cedar closet. The smells emanating from this told McDonough it was a meat-smoker. The place was rich with smells and warmth. They took off their coats and sat while an old black woman poured coffee.

'Thank you, Sarah,' Helen said.

'That boy coming in for supper?'

'He'll drag his tail in soon. Best get food on the table.'

Sarah cast a woeful eye over McDonough, her dark face imbued with a perpetual scowl, as if she looked at life as a dirty trick being played on unsuspecting fools. Her hair was shot through with gray. She was hunched and wrinkled, but her bare arms rippled with strength. Her eyes were bright and alert. She was both intelligent and cunning, McDonough decided.

He nodded his thanks and received a disdainful huff in return.

'I see we's picking up strays again, Miss Helen.'

'Sarah, this is Mr McDonough. He's going to work the winter for us.'

'Uh-huh.' Sarah turned away and began puttering at the stove.

'I'm sorry about Sven, Rafe.'

McDonough shrugged. 'I suppose the boy didn't get along with Gregory either.'

Helen laughed in a pleasant, throaty way.

'No, he did not,' she said. 'Sven saw through Gregory right away. He helped chase him off my range. He's quite handy, really.'

'Seems I should know more about Gregory, seeing as how he and I are linked, at least in most people's minds.'

'You wouldn't be if you'd gotten rid of that hat.'

'Why don't you tell me more about the man.'

'Not much to tell,' she said, sipping at the scalding coffee. 'He didn't work out is all. Some men can't work for a woman. They get ideas about taking over. I wasn't about to let that happen. My dad built all of this. He brought Sarah and me out here, when I was just a baby, soon after my mother died. He started with nothing, built everything himself. When he died he had land from Mendip Creek out to the hills and half-way to town. He had cows and horses, and he had me to leave it to when he passed. He raised me to run this place and I aim to.'

McDonough looked up and down the length of the table. 'Looks like you used to have more hands to feed.'

Helen's face hardened a little.

'Used to. Like I said. Some men have a problem working for a woman. You aren't that kind of man, are you, Rafe?'

'No, I'm not.'

She sighed with relief and smiled. 'I'm glad. I didn't think you were.' Her right hand fell across McDonough's and pressed it warmly. 'Let's never mind about Gregory, all right? He's in the past. A terrible mistake. And not the first I've made. I want to look toward the future. I feel I can do that with you, Rafe.'

The cookhouse door popped open and Sven walked in with an armload of firewood. Silently he kicked the door closed then stepped around the table to drop the wood by the stove. When he returned to the table he sat and slowly removed his coat. Never once did he take his eyes off the spot on the table where Helen held McDonough's hand. His gaze burned into that spot and stayed there long after Helen had withdrawn her hand.

They ate silently, Sven dark and surly. In the bunkhouse later McDonough had his choice of beds. The howling wind lulled him to sleep. In the morning Sven took McDonough to the barn where they saddled horses and rode out into the sluggish herd, Sven on a brown gelding a few hands too short for him and McDonough on the gray mare he had rescued. A smaller horse, this one would handle better than Red chasing after cattle.

In silence they worked for two hours, rotating the herd, bringing tired stock in to feed. Helen came out of the main house and began chipping at the ice on the water-troughs. The cows were greedy for water and she had to ease them away after a time to allow others to drink. Getting in amid the herd she helped rotate them forward.

She looked up and saw McDonough and Sven working at different ends of the herd, each man gently nudging the animals this way and that. They had gotten into a rhythm, these two, the work softening Sven's animosity.

A noise caught her by surprise and she whirled to see two wolves stalking the yard. Glancing back she saw that McDonough had spotted the wolves and was edging his way through the herd. He had taken his rifle from the saddle boot but was in a bad position for a shot.

The cows hadn't seen the wolves yet. Helen faced the brutes, drawing a small revolver from her pocket. A thirty-two caliber Colt Rainmaker. It wouldn't make much noise, but if she could wound or kill one of the wolves the other might flee.

Carefully she aimed and squeezed the trigger. Instantly one of the wolves jerked, its legs flying out from beneath it, and dropped to the snow with a yelp. The second wolf froze, snarling. Helen fired again and hit the beast squarely in the head. It dropped, dead. The first animal got to all fours and began hobbling away. Helen fired again and the wolf toppled over with a thud.

The popping sound of the little gun and the smell of fresh blood started the herd fidgeting. McDonough began singing to them, his voice soft but tuneless. After a few minutes of nervous movement, the animals settled. They were too cold and hungry to stampede.

'Good shooting,' McDonough said, riding up to her. There was surprise in his voice, and admiration. Helen drank it in.

'I think my father wanted a boy,' she said, smiling nervously. 'But I guess he was happy enough with me.'

'I'll take care of the carcasses,' he said, dismounting.

She watched him work for a minute, appreciating his economy of motion, his sureness. After a time they heard the clank of a pot being slapped. Sarah was calling them in to breakfast.

Helen sat at the head of the table this morning with the two men on either side of her. They ate quickly, silently, then settled back for another cup of coffee.

'Looks like a few more have strayed since yesterday,' Helen said.

'Sure, it does,' Sven agreed.

'Well, after we're done I want you boys to go round 'em up. Rafe, why don't you head west toward Mendip Creek then work your way south a bit to the hills; Sven, you go east to Caleb's Nob then head north. See what we can pick up.'

'How will I know the creek?' McDonough asked.

'Is got vater in it,' Sven said, his face puckered into a disdainful scowl.

Helen grinned. 'It's also frozen,' she added. 'But if you head west it's the first creek you get to. Even with the snow it shouldn't be hard to find.'

McDonough let the boy's comment go as good-natured ribbing, which it wasn't. Sven was very protective of Helen and had taken an instant dislike to McDonough, even beyond his reflexive reaction to seeing Gregory's hat and horse. McDonough wondered what had passed between the two, what Gregory had done to earn such enmity.

Saddling their horses again after breakfast, McDonough told the boy:

'I'm not Gregory.' He was cinching Red's saddle, watching Sven out of the corner of his eye. The boy continued to work as if he hadn't heard. When Sven eventually spoke his voice was tight, controlled.

'You wear his hat, his coat. You ride his horse.'

51

'True. But that don't make me him.'

'How did you get his t'ings? Hmm? You kill him?'

'I didn't kill him.'

Sven turned his head slowly and looked McDonough squarely in the eye. He was reading into what McDonough said, or, rather, hadn't said. His eyes narrowed, but he looked confused.

'He vas bad. Killing is vhat he needed.'

'That's a hard thing to say about a man.'

Sven nodded gravely. 'Yah.'

'Did you know him much?'

Shrugging, Sven said: 'He talked. I didn't listen to a t'ing he said. He alvays talked.'

'He talk a lot to Miss Cormier?'

The pale-skinned Swede instantly turned red, looking like a pot-bellied stove ready to blow.

'Too much!' he said through gritted teeth. 'You vork now!'

In a flash Sven threw himself onto the brown gelding and raced out of the barn. McDonough sighed, shaking his head. The boy had so much anger bottled up inside him. Big as he was, McDonough thought, he didn't want to be in Sven's way when he eventually burst.

There was no trail heading west, just a vast open plain covered with rolling mounds of snow. Red picked his way easily over the terrain, pausing now and again to snort or sniff the air, to read the landscape. McDonough sensed disappointment in the animal, as if it realized that in better weather it could run free and easy in such an open place.

After a while he spotted the snow-covered ruts of wagon tracks. These meandered and McDonough would have abandoned them but they maintained a generally westward course. An hour or so later he came to the creek. He dismounted and used the heel of his boot to crack through the thin ice that had formed. Underneath, water flowed sluggishly. He let Red drink sparingly. Surveying the range, he saw little movement. A hawk wheeled overhead, eyeing some far-off meal. There were several dark dots on the horizon that he took for cattle. Too far away to be Box-J brand. In this cold, the animals would not have wandered very far.

For the better part of an hour he walked Red, following the gentle curves of Mendip Creek to the south, letting the animal rest. Hills covered with pine and dotted with bare aspen rose up before him, sharply defined in the frigid, clear air. After a while, he mounted again and pushed Red faster. The chill air was beginning to cut through to his bones.

Mendip Creek curved eastward suddenly. McDonough crossed, letting Red find his own footing, and continued on toward the hills. He had spotted a dark mass at the hill base and reckoned right that it was cattle. The bunch – eight sad-looking brown steers – stood huddled together for warmth over a patch of dirt that had long since been eaten bare. They were a forlorn group, tired and too cold to think. Each wore a Box-J brand.

McDonough choused them gently and they turned east as directed. It would be a long couple of hours before he got them back to the ranch, but they would all make it before dinner.

The pale sun glinted suddenly in McDonough's right eye, flashed once and then again. Instinctively, he threw himself from his saddle, slipping the Spencer from its scabbard in the same motion. With a thud he flopped onto the unforgiving ground and lay there quietly, waiting. But no shots came.

Another glint caught his attention. A glare like quicksilver flashed on Red's saddle two or three times, then disappeared. Cautiously, McDonough rose up using the cattle to shield him. He put the Spencer across the back of one of the animals, sighting along its heavy barrel. There was movement up in the hills. Squinting, he could see a man covered in a hairy coat looking like a shaggy bear. He pulled at the reins of a loaded-down pack-mule. Something glinted along the mule's side. A pot, probably, or maybe a pan.

Small against the hill, the shaggy man hurriedly ascended, crossed behind a stand of trees, and disappeared down the other side. A miner, McDonough thought. A gold-panner, probably. Harmless, but if he was on Box-J land he was stealing. McDonough made a note to come back after delivering the steers and roust the man.

He had just returned the Spencer when a shot rang out from behind him. McDonough turned, pulling at the rifle again, and saw half a dozen riders coming on hard, their approach muffled by the snow. The cattle scattered leaving him alone with Red and no cover from gunplay. Sensing McDonough's thoughts, the lead rider held up a hand and slowed the group to a walk. All of the men wore guns at their hips, but only one of them had his out. This one had fired the shot. A warning shot, McDonough decided, lowering his rifle.

'You're like to scare a fella into throwin' lead,' McDonough told them.

The lead rider grunted and turned toward the man with revolver in his hand.

'Put it away, Zeb.'

Zeb didn't argue. He didn't look to care one way or another.

'You're on Forester land, mister. Name's Adam Felcher and I ramrod this outfit. What're you doing here?'

'Rounding up Box-J cows. They've been wandering. I'm

working for Miss Cormier.'

Two of the men sniggered. Felcher's eyebrow rose with curiosity.

'That a fact? You must be the new man in town Mr Forester talked about. He's been wanting a word with you.'

'He had his chance and decided otherwise. Besides, I've got to get these cows back home.'

'They'll keep,' Felcher said.

McDonough thought for a minute, sizing up Felcher and the men riding with him.

'Thought the fella ramroding Forester's outfit was named Gibson.'

Felcher tightened at the mention of the name.

'He takes care of things around the ranch house. I'm in charge of the stock and the range.'

With a sly smile peeking out the corners of his mouth, McDonough asked:

'Does he do the wash, too?'

Some of the men that had snickered at him now grinned at this insult to Gibson.

'He's not somebody you want to cross, mister,' Felcher said drily. 'Now, are you coming?'

McDonough swiveled his head around a bit to see that the cows had bunched up again for warmth but had taken no further steps toward getting themselves home. They'd keep, and he had questions to ask of Forester.

'Let's go,' he told Felcher as he swung aboard Red and tossed the Spencer into its scabbard.

From the other side of the forested hill, unseen by McDonough, Felcher, and the others, a hairy ball of a man watched the confrontation below through an old-fashioned telescoping spyglass. He had half-buried himself in snow when he doubled back to see if McDonough would follow him. He was sure the man in the sombrero had seen him. It was just his dumb luck to stumble on another body out on this hellishly cold day.

He wasn't a big man, this ball of hair. He stood maybe five-seven, but he was wide and his arms and legs were thick and muscled. He wore a great beard that was shot through with gray and red and matted with meat juices and gristle. He stank with odors emanating from his body, from his beard, and from the bearhide coat he wore.

When the man in the sombrero left with the others – it couldn't be *him*, could it? – he climbed down the hill to his overburdened mule and pulled urgently at the animal's reins. Quickly, they made their way along a game trail squeezed between hills topped by craggy mounds of snow-dusted rock. After a time they came to a well-hidden cave and entered.

The cave mouth appeared undisturbed, ancient, but inside it was deep and obvious that the man lived here. He had made a comfortable bivouac of straw and had built a shielded fire-pit that still smoldered. There was hay in the corner for the mule, a pool of water dripping out of the rock wall, a coal-oil lamp, and a makeshift shelf with a half-dozen dog-eared, moldy books.

The hairy man wasted no time uncovering a stash of small cloth sacks, most of them stuffed full. He took a half-empty sack from his coat pocket and added it to the cache, then secreted them again beneath a slab of granite.

He looked over at the mule, grinning beneath his matted beard, and laughed hoarsely.

'Soon, Lucifer. Soon you an' ol' Robaire will have what we came fer an' we can git out of this hell-hole.'

Forester's ranch was more modest than McDonough

expected. It was built low to the ground and sprawled only a little. The only thing grandiose about it was the enormous porch that wrapped around three sides of the house. Eight men could sit front to back on that porch and have room for a floorshow, McDonough observed.

He was guided beneath the arch of an open gate which had a triangle burned into the wood, an R at its center and a P below it. McDonough dismounted with the others and took the Spencer and his saddle bags. He was being rude, but he felt no compunction over it. He was, after all, to his way of thinking, being kidnapped.

A man waited on the porch in shirtsleeves and a vest. He was older, perhaps sixty and wore a trimmed white beard over a weather-reddened face. His torso was like a molasses barrel, heavy and thick around. Forester. He didn't look pleased to see McDonough.

'Come into the house,' he growled.

Felcher nodded to the others and they faded away into the bunkhouse. Then he used his chin to point McDonough toward the house. There was a moment's hesitation as he wondered if he had stepped into a trap. But he decided Forester wouldn't be the kind to kill in his own home, so he climbed the steps and crossed the great divide, through the front door, and into a large room filled with heavy furniture.

'You'll miss your dinner,' Forester said. 'So we'll have a meal together.' He had taken a place beside a large leather wingback chair, posed stiffly, as if for a photographer, a large fire roaring behind him in a great stone fireplace.

'Is that an invitation?' McDonough asked, placing his belongings on the floor.

Forester puffed out his chest and released a great gust of breath.

'I don't know where you're from, son, maybe back East where things are proper and manners are smooth. I'm not. That was an invitation.'

McDonough grinned. 'Could use a meal.'

Forester glared for a minute.

'So, you've hired on with Helen Cormier,' he said.

'Is there a problem with that?' Forester had not asked him to sit down, which suited McDonough. He didn't like the idea of the rancher towering over him.

'Not at all. Helen's all right. Not the cowman her father was, and maybe she hasn't got enough sense to know when to quit, but you working for her doesn't cause me lack of sleep.' He pointed at the sheepskin coat and sombrero. 'Those, however, do.'

'You're not alone in that.'

'I want to know how you came by those things.' His tone was commanding. He meant to have his answer.

McDonough shrugged. 'I could have picked them up in Bowman a few weeks back. Cold country up there in the Dakotas.'

Even before he finished talking Forester was shaking his head.

'You know I won't believe that.'

Gibson stepped into the room. He purposely avoided looking at McDonough and instead addressed Forester.

'Food's up.'

Out of his heavy coat, Gibson looked even larger than McDonough had remembered. Every inch of Gibson was compacted into pure muscle and tendon and bone. His hands flexed in agitation. The mop of black hair on his head and thick eyebrows added to the man's devilish appearance.

Once he had delivered his message, he backed out of

the room. But his gaze wavered for a split second and he glared blackly at McDonough before disappearing down the hall.

'Let's eat,' Forester said, himself already half-way out of the room.

They passed down another corridor to a dining-hall that would easily accommodate twenty diners around a huge central mahogany table. The furniture was polished to a mirrorlike sheen. Extra chairs and cabinets lined the room. Large lifelike paintings of ranch scenes hung on two of the walls.

Covered food trays were arranged at one end of the table. Forester sat and motioned for McDonough to take the seat next to him. The big rancher did not stand on ceremony. He piled his plate high with slabs of meat and bread and began eating. McDonough took a more modest portion for himself.

Gibson meanwhile had stationed himself against the wall behind and to the left of Forester, between the rancher and his guest, giving himself clear view of McDonough.

Pausing in his chewing, Forester said:

'I'll take that answer now.'

McDonough considered his words for a few moments.

'The other day you said you weren't interested.'

'Today I am.'

'Why?'

Forester put down his fork, his face darkening with anger.

'I don't like Gregory.'

'Most people I've met don't. It means nothing to me.'

McDonough heard soft footsteps behind him and saw Forester shake his head quickly. A tingle ran down McDonough's spine. He had left his rifle in the other room so he held onto the fork in his hand tightly, not eating, just waiting.

'If that's true,' Forester said, 'then you won't mind answering my question.'

But he did mind, McDonough realized. He minded because this was something Forester wanted, apparently more than anything else. He minded, too, because while it had been the source of his troubles since arriving in town the information was also his ace in the hole. Or so he thought.

'I got it from Gregory,' he said at last with a shrug.

Forester leaned forward. 'How?'

'Well, let's just say he didn't object.'

'He didn't mind you taking his horse, either, I gather.'

'Not hardly.'

Forester nodded. 'So he's dead, then. You kill him?'

'No. Someone with a deep mad gunned him. Four shots. Looked like he had been beaten recently, too.'

'A lot of folks hated that man.' Forester shrugged. 'Not surprised.'

'Not a lot of people I've met could have given that beating.'

Again anger flared in Forester. 'I don't need to beat men to get what I want.'

'Not when there are those so willing to do it for you.' McDonough glanced up at Gibson standing against the wall like a rabid animal waiting to lash out. Forester didn't turn around but he ducked his head slightly with an involuntary glance back over his shoulder. His body sagged a bit, reluctantly and silently admitting the truth. Then he looked past McDonough and tossed his head in a quick motion. Whoever it was who had come up from behind turned and walked away.

'It's not what you think,' he said, quietly.

'Sure it is.'

'I'm concerned about the men Helen hires. Gregory had worked for her for a few months before coming to me looking for a job. He didn't like working for a woman, he said, especially one that 'rodded her own outfit. I understood that and took him on. It was a mistake.'

Now that his confession had started, Forester didn't seem able to stop. It made him uncomfortable. He stood and walked away from the table to stare at one of the paintings hanging on the wall.

'This is my home, Mr McDonough. Came out here in 'forty-six when there was nothing. Wouldn't bring a woman into this place so I never married. All I've got is the ranch and I don't like men what try to take it, or any piece of it from me. I've fought Indians and rustlers and fool men who thought they could talk me out of my land. I can see that kind coming from a long way off. I should have seen it in Gregory, but I didn't.'

'A rustler?'

Forester laughed. 'If he was, he was the worst kind! I swear that man was a fool. Took about a hundred head and kept them in a hollow back of the hills. My men found them with no trouble.'

'That don't answer my question.'

'Gregory left town a few days ago,' the rancher said, coming back to the table and sitting. 'I thought you were sent as a decoy while he worked his way back onto my range to try and steal more cattle.'

'He must have thought little of you if he believed a hat and coat would lead you to distraction.'

'Fact is, it did. That's when I came into town and met you.' Forester ignored McDonough's wry smile at the

61

mention of that meeting. 'I hate Gregory. Him leaving was the best thing for everyone, otherwise I don't know what I would have done. The old ways aren't completely gone out here, you know.'

'So, I'm his accomplice, is that it?'

'He had one. Saw sign of it up in the hills but could never track it down.'

'Well, I'm new to the territory, so you can forget about that. I never laid eyes on Gregory 'til he was dead. You say he left town a few days ago?'

'About a day or two before the storm. We don't know exactly. It's big country, but I figure that was the last anyone saw him. He was in town about then, got some supplies, then rode out.'

'Just pulled up stakes?'

'I caught him rustling,' Forester admitted. 'Gave him a choice: a jail cell or the road. He took the road.'

McDonough shoved a last piece of bread into his mouth and swallowed the rest of his coffee. He pushed back the heavy padded chair, stood and took the sombrero from the table where he had placed it.

'Mind if I ask a personal question?' The rancher nodded his head tightly. 'You don't have family, so what happens to your ranch when you've gone?'

Confusion lacing his voice, Forester said: 'Gibson'll buy me out when it's time. He's been like a son to me.'

McDonough nodded. 'I reckon he's got a lot to protect, then, doesn't he? Just like you do.'

CHAPTER FIVE

He got back to the Box-J before sunset with thoughts of Gregory's accomplice nettling him. If there was such a man, and he was still in the hills, he might know of Clara, a name that had quickly become an obsession with him. At some point, he'd have to go looking for this mystery man.

McDonough left the strays he'd collected with the rest of the herd. Sven was setting out bales of hay and cycling the cattle over to the watering troughs where Helen busily chipped away at the ice. Silently, McDonough saw to unsaddling his horse then went out to help Helen and Sven. They worked until dark.

From the cookhouse Sarah banged on a pot and bellowed that supper was on.

'I vill put these bales avay,' Sven said, hefting one of the awkward bundles and trudging off toward the barn. The boy hadn't said a word or even looked at McDonough since he returned.

McDonough nodded to Helen. 'We'll catch up.'

She smiled, veiled relief crossing her face, then went to the cookhouse. McDonough lifted one of the bales, struggling to balance it, and brought it into the barn.

'Where do you want this?' he asked Sven.

'I'll do it.'

'Sure. But where do I put this one?'

Sven gestured to a corner where several other bales had been stacked. McDonough dropped his on top of another and shoved it even.

'Kind of awkward,' he said.

'Your arms are too short,' Sven told him.

McDonough held out his arms to examine them. Shorter than Sven's, that was for certain. Sven went back outside and scooped up another bale. McDonough followed, took a bale of his own, and trailed the boy back inside. This went on in silence for several minutes until all the bales were under cover and stacked up.

'The others don't work so hard,' Sven said. He was looking at the wall of hay-bales they had just made, picking at the stray stalks that stuck up like wild hairs.

'Hard work keeps me warm.'

'Yah.'

Together they crossed the compound to the cookhouse. Helen had already started eating. Plates were on the table awaiting the men. The meal was a silent one, but there wasn't much of a dark cloud hanging over the table. Eating was serious business to a cowhand. Talk came later after the food was gone.

'You get here on time,' Sarah scolded, 'your food'll be hot.'

After the meal, Sven brought his plate to the wash-tub and mumbled thanks to Sarah. The old black woman looked up at the boy who towered over her and smiled bright and motherly at him. Reaching up she patted his cheek.

'Your lessons, I think now, boy,' she told him. He blushed a little, self-consciously ducking his head toward McDonough. 'Go on.'

Sven said his goodnights and hurried from the room.

'Learning that boy to read,' Sarah told McDonough. 'He needs encouragement, not cowpoke harrying.'

'Won't say a word,' he promised.

Sarah looked unconvinced as she took a plate of food and went out toward the main house.

'She prefers eating at the house,' Helen explained. 'The cookhouse is for the hands, she says.'

'You've probably a fine dining-room. You should use it.'

Shaking her head, Helen said, 'That's what Sarah says. But I can't. My father ate his meals here because he worked the ranch like any of his hands. I won't do less.'

McDonough got up to retrieve the coffee-pot.

'There's no shame in getting help with the place,' he said as he filled their cups.

Her eyes flared. 'I'll run it my way. I won't give up the Box-J just because a man thinks he can run it better.'

'Not what I meant. You could use a couple more hands, is all.'

'Well, that's a problem. Hands cost money, and money's a bit tight.'

'You've got a good spread here. A fair number of cows. This fall you should be able to sell a chunk of that herd for a good profit.'

Helen sniffed derisively. 'If I can get them to market. And if I can get them there before Forester.'

'Yeah,' McDonough nodded. 'He's got a big outfit.'

'The biggest. He's got the army beef contract and he's usually first in line with the Eastern cattle buyers and gets the best prices. He's got more men and cows than the rest of us put together.'

She was starting to feel sorry for herself. McDonough could hear it in her voice and it made him uncomfortable.

Suddenly she shook herself and laughed.

'Well, I wanted to be a cowman!' she said. 'We do all right. And one day we'll do better. This land is too good for me to fail.'

Her smile was bright and cheerful. She got up and moved around the table to sit next McDonough. He could see in her eyes, though, that a hint of despair lingered. Then he felt her hand on his, warm and soft and feminine. There were calluses on her fingers, but even these felt dainty and smooth.

Looking up at him she said: 'Thanks for listening, Rafe. I don't usually let it get to me. But sometimes . . . well, it's good to have a man to talk to.'

She was very close. How she had edged nearer to him, he didn't know. He felt the heat of her closeness through her plaid workshirt, saw the rise and fall of her well-formed bosom. Her breath came in rapid, short gasps. Her lips were so near all he had to do was lean forward and take them. Part of him ached to respond, his mind screaming to kiss her. But it was the quiet voice he listened to, the one that warned him of danger.

'It's been a long day,' he said, standing. 'I need to turn in.'

Helen started as if waking from a day-dream, looking up at him with moist eyes. She took a moment to steady her breathing.

'Sleep well,' she told him coolly.

More cattle had wandered off during the night. McDonough and Sven spent much of the morning rounding them up, this time together. There had been a clear trail left in some fresh snow that had fallen overnight, and the pair were able to track down the more than a dozen strays that had gotten away.

The two didn't talk much, but they worked well together. Sven was a natural horseman and he rode easily and with pride. McDonough found himself admiring the boy. With his ability and confidence Sven would be a top hand one day, and soon.

After they nooned back at the ranch, Helen came up and told them about the supplies she had ordered, that they were ready and needed to be picked up. It appeared to McDonough that she wanted Sven to volunteer. The youth remained mute, reluctant to leave the ranch and his protective watch on Helen. Shear stubbornness prevented McDonough from volunteering so he waited for Helen to grow frustrated and make a choice. She looked embarrassed when she asked McDonough to do it.

With the new snow, it was impossible to drive a buckboard into town. McDonough roped six horses and fitted them with pack saddles. He laced the reins together to the end of a good rope and looped the other end around Red's saddle horn. Red was a strong horse. They'd follow him.

Leaving so late in the day, and the trail being difficult, he knew he would arrive in Sprigensguth around sundown. That would give him time to see to the horses and meet with Mr Rumpskin before he closed up the general store to ensure the order would be ready in the morning. Helen had wanted to save money on a hotel room, but the supplies were needed. It was, she said, just one more thing nibbling away at her.

There had been a look in her eyes when she gave instructions to McDonough. It took him about five miles of cold road and slow walking to figure out what it was that he had seen in that look. She was worried. About what, he couldn't say. She had made her intentions fairly plain to him last night yet he had rejected her. At least that was the way it appeared to her. But he hadn't rejected her. She had moved too fast for him; and he wasn't used to kissing the boss. So maybe, he thought, she was worried he would run off. But there was little chance of that. This late in the season he was lucky to have a job, three squares, and a warm place to sleep. He wasn't about to leave even these Spartan comforts. And although she didn't know it, he needed to resolve the question of the woman Clara before he moved on.

The sun was a distant orange ball as McDonough tramped into town past the Plains Café. He glanced over at the large windows but could see little more than ghostly shapes through the frost-covered panes. Patrons had rubbed a few of the glass squares clean of ice and in one of these was framed the long, handsome face of Adele Chappell. She was looking toward someone, a small smile on her lips and a sparkle in her eyes. Her smile broadened as she turned from the frame.

The liveryman was not pleased to see McDonough, but he took the seven horses and put them in stalls with oats and hay. McDonough paid the man in advance and told him to have the animals ready at sun-up. Head down and buried in the sombrero, he crossed the street and went down the block to the general store to arrange for an early morning pick-up of Helen's order. He bought a few cigars from the quivering Rumpskin then left to visit Adele.

The café was not as busy as it had been earlier when he passed by on his way into town. A few diners lingered over their coffee, not eager to brave the cold. Adele saw him as soon as he entered and rushed over to him. She led him to a table away from the others and sat with him. He couldn't mistake the pleasure she had in seeing him again. His heartbeat quickened a little as he looked at her.

'Didn't think I'd ever see you again,' she said, 'especially not so soon.'

'Need some supplies,' he said.

'She didn't have to send you. There's Sven, too.'

'Flipped a coin I guess,' he told her. 'I got the wrong side.'

For a moment her eyes widened and her face lost a little color.

'You didn't want to come?' But she saw his grin and chided him with a slap to the wrist.

She fed him, then. Chicken, steak, an entire loaf of homemade bread, a full pot of coffee, and three pieces of canned cherry pie. Other customers had come in and demanded some of her time. She stole minutes to return to him and talk. At last he stood to leave.

'I'd best be getting over to the hotel and get a room for the night,' he told her.

She pressed close.

'I'll be closing up soon,' she said. 'After you get your room why don't you come over to my house for some coffee. Didn't have much time to talk while you were eating.'

'Eating is serious business, ma'am,' he informed, with mock gravity.

'I've seen that.'

He ducked his head a little, no longer pretending seriousness.

'I don't think I ought to, Adele. I know what small towns are like. Bound to set some tongues a-waggin'.'

'Anyone out on a night like this hasn't any business casting stones, Rafe. Come over for coffee and dessert. Please.'

'Dessert, too? Woman, I'm stuffed to the rafters as it is.'

'Coffee, then.'

He hesitated only a little before answering:

'Thank you. I will.'

The whiskey hadn't done what Danvers said it would. Albert Mendall was colder than he should have been, shivering so that his teeth were chattering. Danvers said the whiskey would warm him and it had burned going down. Sitting in the saloon, the alcohol sloshing around in his stomach, he had felt a flush ripple through him and the heat rise up out of his mouth as he exhaled. The boys had chipped in to buy him three shots of Danvers' best – the stuff he kept under the bar behind the shotgun. But now in the shadow of Benton's haberdashery he felt his fingers and toes going numb with cold. They had offered him a hot-water bottle, too, and he cursed himself now for not taking it.

He'd heard that Dick Gregory, that sidewinding thief, had come back to town. And after that beating he'd taken, too. Well, Gregory had oysters, that was for sure. Someone said it wasn't really Gregory, but Pete assured him it was. Same hat, same coat, same mean temper. Mendall's stomach turned at the thought of Pete's hand. It was bad, all swollen and black. It would have to come off but Pete wouldn't hear of it. Poor Pete. Well, Gregory was as good as dead. He'd gun him down for old Pete.

Nearly an hour had passed and Mendall's resolve had nearly evaporated when a light shone in the doorway of the café. A big man carrying a rifle stood framed in the door. Adele leaned in close to him, looking up with a smile on her face. That was strange. Gregory had tried to make time with Adele before and she'd have none of it. Well, women! Who could figure them.

The man in Gregory's coat and hat nodded to Adele then turned and made his way to the opposite side of the street, to the boardwalk and then up the street toward the hotel. Mendall swore silently. He thought Gregory would go back to the stables first. Now the shot would be harder.

Mendall raised his revolver, his arm leaden, his hand frozen as if in a block of ice. He just needed to pull the trigger once, he told himself. Just one clean shot.

Gregory was in the shadows of the shop awnings, the moon casting an uncertain glow over the town. He paused at the edge of one walkway. Below by two steps was another stretch of boardwalk, more shops, and a narrow alley between buildings. A small light flared as he struck a match and lit a cigar. For an instant, the tiny flame lighted his face. Mendall fired.

Gregory went down and rolled, his hat flying off his head. Caught by the wind the sombrero flipped over and followed Gregory to the lower boardwalk.

Mendall whooped and started to turn down the alley between the haberdasher's and the barbershop when he saw Gregory get to his feet and, hunched over, run toward the hotel. Whipping his gun around Mendall fired two quick shots. Across the street a plate-glass window broke and wood splintered.

Gregory ducked into a narrow alley, letting the blackness swallow him. Mendall expected return fire but none came. He waited, himself covered in shadows, ready to fire again. Minutes passed and he began to shiver. Cold had flooded back into him after the rush of excitement. But it was more than that. Staring at the black alley across the street, terror began to creep into his bones.

If he left now, all that Gregory would know was that

someone had taken a shot at him. That someone hated him enough to kill him. Well, that sidewinder already knew that. But he wouldn't know who had fired those shots, and Mendall could keep him from finding out if he could just get back to Danvers' place without being seen.

Mendall pocketed the gun, eased down the alley and carefully made his way back to the saloon. Along the way he met no one, saw no one. When he pushed into the safety of the saloon he was flooded with warmth and relief.

Danvers stood at the bar cleaning glasses. Pete was with him, cradling his arm. The man looked close to tears. He had just downed a shot of whiskey and slapped the glass against the bar for more. At Mendall's entrance he looked up sharply.

'Well?' he demanded.

Mendall rushed toward the bar and let the revolver slip out of his hand and clatter against the worn, unpolished wood.

'Give me a whiskey, Danvers. And I'll take that hot-water bottle now.' Mendall flexed his fingers, grimacing in pain.

'Blast you!' Pete bellowed. 'I asked you a question.'

'Hit him, I think.'

'You think?'

'He went down for a minute.' Mendall grabbed the shot-glass that Danvers had just filled and tossed its contents down his throat. It burned, worse than the aged stuff the boys had staked him to earlier, but he welcomed the heat none the less. A rubber bottle slapped against the bar and Mendall took it in hand, cradling it gratefully.

'You should have made sure.'

Mendall shook his head. 'Weren't gonna foller him down no dark alley, Pete. Not fer three shots of whiskey. You'll get yerself another chance.'

From behind him, Mendall heard the front door slam and a heavy boot fall on the floor. The whiskey turned to ice in his stomach. He could see Pete shaking, not with fear but with rage. With slow movements Mendall turned. He kept his hands loose but in plain view.

'I'm looking for a fella that misplaced some bullets,' the tall man in Gregory's coat said. The man had a rifle in one hand – a Spencer – and a long-barreled Remington revolver in the other. Mendall's stomach turned again. This wasn't Gregory and for a moment, looking into the stranger's dark face, Mendall wished it were.

Standing in the middle of the doorway of Danvers' Retreat, McDonough looked about the saloon for a small-caliber gun. He spat out the cigar clamped between his teeth, concentrating all his anger in that violent gesture. Only a few minutes ago he had been in excellent spirits and had lit the smoke in celebration. He held the Spencer casually, almost daring someone to draw on him.

There were six men in the saloon including the bartender. He recognized Pete from their earlier dust-up. He saw the man's hand and wrist, black and purple and dead looking, and felt a twinge of regret over causing such an injury. But Pete had begun the argument and, dead hand or not, it looked as if he was ready to continue with it.

Looking at the dirty collection of wastrels and drunks gathered in the gloom, McDonough knew his bush-whacker was here. Each man was armed and McDonough was thankful he'd strapped on the Remington before leaving the Box-J.

Three men sat at a table by one of the stoves. These would be no trouble, McDonough decided. They darted anxious glances up toward Pete.

It was the other three he'd have to worry about.

Pete had let go his blackened hand, wincing as he did it, and let his good hand fall slowly to the gun strapped to his hip. Danvers was scowling as he inched his left shoulder down toward the bar. He could have been preparing to duck if shooting started but McDonough didn't think so. The bartender was reaching for a weapon. The third man stood closest to McDonough, shivering, holding a hot-water bottle in his hands, with a look of terror in his eyes. The man was dangerously near panicking. Within reach of his hand was a gun. It looked like a McWorter .38. A small caliber gun.

'That yours?' McDonough asked, tossing a look at the gun on the bar. Mendall couldn't answer for shivering. He swallowed hard.

'I said—'

'Yes!'

McDonough nodded. 'I think you may have left some cartridges on the street.'

'Not me, mister.' A light had ignited behind Mendall's terror-filled eyes. 'Ain't fired the thing in weeks.' With a shaking hand, he reached back toward the revolver. 'Let me show you.'

'Don't,' McDonough said softly, already regretting the outcome.

'Let me show you,' Mendall repeated, his voice quivering.

Mendall dropped the water bottle and in the same instant swept the revolver into his hand and spun on his heels. Shaking with fear he let his first shot go too early. It twanged off the barrel of the stove at the front of the saloon, ricocheted and smashed window glass. McDonough fired one shot. Mendall doubled over, struck in the belly. The McWorter cracked again, slapping lead into the floor.

Another shot boomed and McDonough felt a tug at his sleeve. Whipping the Remington around, he fired two quick shots into Pete. The man screamed and fell dead.

'Don't,' McDonough warned the bartender with a hard, sideways glance. Danvers froze then slowly lifted his empty hands to the bar.

On the floor Mendall was crying as he tried to crawl toward his revolver. Within inches of his fingers, it seemed like miles away. He was cold, so cold, and his belly burned. It had been burning all night, with one thing or another. He hated that feeling.

A boot fell onto his hand, crushing his fingers. He hardly felt it. Looking up he saw the tall man wearing Gregory's coat and hat.

'You ain't Gregory,' Mendall wheezed.

'No.'

Mendall relaxed and the man removed his boot.

'I thought . . . Pete said. . . .'

'Pete was a fool.'

'Well, hell, so was I.' Mendall coughed out a chuckle and died.

Looking over the others in the saloon, McDonough saw that none of them wanted to take a hand in this. He was about to back out when the front door opened and something like a sledgehammer hit him square between the shoulders.

CHAPTER SIX

McDonough shot forward, propelled by the blow, and slammed against the floor. The Remington skittered off, but his left hand had been wrapped around the Spencer's receiver tightly. When he slammed against the floor, his fingers were crushed under the rifle. He let out a yelp of pain and surprise.

'I'm gonna kill ya, ya dog!'

McDonough rolled to find Forester's man Strap Gibson standing over him, furious and looking for blood. Gibson pulled open his coat, reaching for a gun holstered beneath his armpit. Swinging with the rifle, McDonough clipped Gibson's jaw. The ranch foreman tumbled sideways and fell against the stove even as he struggled to clear his own gun.

McDonough scrambled to his feet and swung again with the rifle. The heavy stock smacked Gibson's hand, sending his revolver sliding across the room. Shifting his balance, McDonough kicked at Gibson who was able only partly to block the blow. Gibson tumbled to the floor, knocking chairs as he fell.

McDonough pivoted, brought the Spencer up to his

shoulder, and fired a shot at the wall behind the bar. The bullet buzzed inches from Danvers' head as the bartender lifted a shotgun.

'I ain't giving you another chance, Danvers.'

Trembling, the bartender nodded quickly as he moved out from behind the bar, leaving the shotgun behind.

Gibson pulled himself to his feet. He felt his jaw with a tender touch.

'What do you want with me?' McDonough asked. 'I thought we squared things with Forester the other day.'

'With him, maybe. But not with me.' Gibson tossed a glance at the floor. His gun was too far away. He'd be gunned down before he could reach it.

'What's your beef? I ain't Gregory.'

'You're as good as.' Gibson wiped the corner of his mouth and came away with a blood-smeared hand. 'I figure you and Gregory are working together. He got his beating and left but he didn't go far. He went to his partner – you – and made plans to sneak back and rustle more Forester beef while you distract everyone.'

'Your beef, you mean.'

'Yeah. Mine.'

McDonough shook his head. 'If you're missing cows that ain't my fault or my problem. Take it up with the constable.'

'The storm put a crimp in your plans,' Gibson accused. 'When it clears up that's when Gregory'll make his move.'

'I told you what happened to Gregory.'

'I don't believe you. I want to know where he is. Now, are you man enough to put that rifle down and let us settle things right?'

McDonough glanced down at the Spencer in his fist, a half-smile playing on his face.

77

'No,' he said. 'Let's go on over to the constable and discuss this.'

'You're gonna have to shoot me, then. 'Cause I'm going for my gun.'

Gibson had a wild look in his eye fueled by hate and greed. Reason had fled him long ago.

McDonough flipped the rifle in a smooth motion and swung it at Gibson. It smacked the foreman's head as he began his dive toward his fallen revolver. With a heavy grunt, Gibson collapsed to the floor, unconscious. Kneeling over the body McDonough felt the man's pulse. It was strong.

He looked up at the others in the saloon, sighed with disgust.

Behind him the saloon door opened and the soft voice of Constable Thackery called:

'Drop the long gun, Mr McDonough. I'd hate to have to plug you.'

The cell in Thackery's jail left much to be desired. The pallet was hard and cold and no amount of blankets could warm him. A stove burned brightly but it was too far across the small room for McDonough's liking. Thackery had given him coffee and a chamber-pot and the hot-water bottle Mendall had dropped. Having no deputy, Thackery spent the night sleeping outside the cell and the policeman's discomfort went only a short distance in taking the edge off of McDonough's own.

In the morning both men were stiff and sore and cold. Silently, Thackery added coal to the stove and put on a fresh pot of coffee.

'You want to tell me about it now?' Thackery asked.

After tossing McDonough in jail the previous night, the

constable had spent a couple of cold hours dealing with the corpses and getting a doctor for Gibson. Once the undertaker had removed the bodies, Thackery returned to the jail to find McDonough asleep in his cell.

Waking to the smell of fresh coffee, McDonough told Thackery of his errand in town for Helen and his supper at the café and the ambush that nearly killed him. He gave details, unvarnished, simple, truthful. Thackery listened.

'So you followed Mendall into the saloon and gunned him down.'

'If that's what the men there are saying, it's a lie.'

'Danvers said you came in shooting.'

McDonough could only shake his head.

'Well, I didn't get much of a chance to talk to the others last night. I'll do that now. Their heads'll be clearer anyway.' Thackery took the coffee-pot and set it on the floor near the cell. 'Adele will be coming by with breakfast soon. Leastways you get good food while you're here.'

Wrapped in two scarves and with his hat plastered down on his head, Constable Thackery left the jail and worked his way to the center of town. Although the day was cold, there were a few more citizens about. Killing and shooting, reflected Thackery, tended to feed curiosity. He paused, looking at the dull entrance to Danvers' Retreat, and mentally shook his head. Danvers had told his story; he wouldn't change it now. Thackery hadn't believed the man. He knew that Danvers had a deep hatred for Gregory; and he knew that Danvers wasn't smart enough to distinguish between the hated ranch hand and the newcomer wearing Gregory's coat. The bartender was about as thick as a clay brick, and a mean cuss who could hold a grudge. But there was more of the stranger's story to check out. Pulling his coat tight about his throat,

Thackery plodded out into the snowy street and got to work.

Inside the jail, McDonough shifted again on his pallet, trying to find a comfortable position. For a moment he considered confessing to murder if it meant he could get a feather-bed for a night. Thackery had been gone nearly half an hour when the jail door opened again and Adele hurried in.

She wore a heavy topcoat and her head was wrapped in a shawl. Beneath that was a pretty green dress, very heavy and layered. She carried a small basket which was also wrapped with a shawl.

She set the basket on the constable's desk.

'I wondered what happened to you last night,' she said. There was a strange play of emotions on her face: anger mixed with relief and colored just a little by suspicion. She looked him in the eye, a steady gaze that patiently waited for explanation yet didn't expect one.

'I ran into some trouble,' he said, getting to his feet.

A flash of color filled her cheeks.

'I can see that.' She was angry, he thought, yet almost smiling. He searched his own emotions wondering why he found that pleasing.

Out of the basket she took a plate of eggs and bacon and half a loaf of bread and slipped them through the feed-slot on the floor.

'They say you killed two men,' she said.

They had both bent low, she to deliver the food, he to accept it. But he didn't touch the plate. Instead he rose to his feet as she stood up again, holding her gaze.

'I had to,' he admitted.

Adele swallowed, then said: 'And you nearly broke a man's jaw.'

This surprised McDonough. He stifled a chuckle.

'Well, how about that.'

'Eat your eggs,' she told him. 'Before they turn to ice.'

She didn't leave. Quietly she pulled Thackery's chair away from the desk and sat. McDonough scooped the plate off the floor and began shoveling food into his mouth. After all he had eaten the previous night he didn't think he would be so ravenous. But Adele's good cooking made him hungry for more.

'Will you talk about it?'

'You told me to get a new coat!'

'Rafe! Please.'

He told her, as he had told Thackery, the unvarnished truth. She listened intently, nodding occasionally. She had heard about Mendall, how weak he was, and about Pete Rigby's hard meanness. Hearing the story, she could visualize how these men had drawn McDonough into a deadly fight.

'Wouldn't've killed either of them if they hadn't pushed it to that point.'

'And Gibson?'

'Oh, I don't like Gibson.'

'Rafe,' she scolded again.

'He took a hand, Adele. Jumped me from behind. I had to fight him off.'

Adele got up and retrieved the plate that McDonough left on the floor. He was still chewing on the last bit of bread and drinking coffee.

As she put the plate back into the basket Adele felt overwhelmed. She flushed, felt her face redden, and knew that tears were forming in her eyes. McDonough saw her sag a little and turn away. He pressed close to the bars, reaching a hand out to her.

'I don't understand,' she said. 'Why are they trying to kill you?'

'They hated Gregory, I guess, and I remind them of him.'

She spun, suddenly angry. 'Then get rid of that coat!'

'I can't now,' he shrugged. 'Wouldn't make a difference anyway. They think I'm here for a reason.'

'And you've been letting them!' she accused.

He had been letting them think that, McDonough realized. He knew why but didn't know if he could put it into words.

'I suppose I have,' he confessed.

Her face a mask of steel, Adele asked:

'How did you come by that hat and coat, Rafe? Please tell me.'

He didn't have to think about it. He told her all of it. Everything about the blizzard and finding Gregory's body and bundling up inside the dead man's clothes to stay alive.

'He hadn't died right away, Adele. He took four gunshots to the body and yet lived long enough to either bleed to death or freeze. That's a hard way to go.'

'What was he to you?'

'Nobody.'

'Then why. . . ?'

'A man out in the world alone like that, nothing he owns but what's on his back, nothing that's his but his pride and his horse. To die like that, bleeding out, hated, left for the coyotes, and with no one to know of your passing. I just couldn't leave it like that, Adele. Gregory was a mean cuss, if what people are saying is true. But he was a man, alive, full of desires and plans, and somebody must've loved him. Whoever that is deserves to know what happened. They *need* to know.'

Adele looked away again as he had spoken, taking in his words. Now she turned back and watched at him closely.

'Who's Clara to you, Rafe?'

A crooked smile twitched on his lips.

'Nothing, Adele. Gregory had started writing a letter to her. It was in his pocket, but there's no address and no one seems to know her.'

Adele stepped close to the bars and reached out.

'I'm sorry, Rafe,' she said.

'For what?'

'Never mind,' she said, shaking her head.

They were both smiling now. McDonough looked down and saw that Adele had laid her hand across his as it rested on the cell bars. It was a warm, comfortable feeling.

'It wasn't you out there, Rafe. That doesn't have to be your end. Not if you don't want it to be.'

They heard footsteps approaching outside, a stuttering scrape as boots climbed the steps. Then the door opened and the cold pushed inside for a second. Helen Cormier closed the door quickly and tossed off her hat and the scarf wrapped around her face. She took in the scene at the cell bars with a strange smile on her face – an odd mix of mocking contempt and anger.

Adele pulled her hand away from McDonough's self-consciously, hating herself for the demure gesture. She wasn't intimidated by Helen, just didn't like her. But something else had made her secretive all of a sudden. It was the stirring of feelings she had for McDonough, a foreign thing to her that she didn't want to admit to herself, let alone to anyone else.

'You're dedicated to your job,' Helen said brightly.

Adele wanted to respond but held her tongue. There

83

was nothing she could say that wouldn't inflame Helen. Standing her ground at the cell, Adele suddenly realized that words *would* inflame Helen. The woman was jealous. Something fluttered in her stomach as she wondered if Rafe had given Helen cause to be jealous.

'Well, I hope you enjoyed breakfast, Rafe. Because you won't get another meal in town.' Helen smiled pleasantly. 'At least not from that jail cell.'

'I don't understand.'

'Constable Thackery is coming now. You're to be released. *Into my custody.* Gibson told what happened and he's not pressing charges. Forester is taking care of any damages.'

Adele let out a sigh, surprised that she had been holding her breath.

'I'm glad, Rafe.'

McDonough turned to the café owner.

'Thanks for breakfast. Sorry I missed that coffee.'

'Another time,' she said turning from the cell door. McDonough reached out and took her hand.

'Real soon,' he promised.

Helen nodded curtly to Adele and watched the woman leave. Before the door could shut Constable Thackery entered.

'You drink up all my coffee?' he asked.

'Every drop.'

Thackery took a set of keys from the desk and unlocked the cell door.

'Should keep you in there just for that. But it looks like your story is the right one.'

'It's the truth,' McDonough said firmly. 'What about the two dead men?'

'Well, I knew about yours and Pete's dust up a few days

84

ago. He's an ornery cuss. And I found Mendall's tracks in the snow and backtrailed him to the spot where he tried to ambush you. Things pretty much line up as you said.'

Thackery handed McDonough his confiscated gunbelt, hat, and coat. 'This is a pretty quiet town. I like it that way. So do most of the folks around here. I don't want to see any more trouble buzzing around you, McDonough.'

'Never came looking for trouble, Constable. Usually run from it.'

McDonough slipped into his coat and shoved the hat down on his head. At the door Helen looked up at him with a scowl that had just a hint of a grin in it.

'You're causing me trouble, Rafe. Maybe I should fire you.'

'Look at it this way, Helen. Getting tossed in jail for the night saved the cost of a hotel room.'

'And breakfast.'

'There was that.'

'Oh, McDonough,' Thackery said. 'I asked around a bit about Clara. Nobody's heard of her. Sorry.'

McDonough tensed at the mention of the mystery woman's name. He looked down at Helen whose curiosity was lit. She worked to keep it from showing but her head was cocked to one side and her eyebrows were arched high up on her forehead.

'Thanks,' McDonough said, opening the door. He eased Helen out of the jail and set a quick pace toward the center of town.

'We'll need to pick up the horses and then head over to the store,' he told her.

'Already done. Who's Clara?'

He paused a moment, looked down at her, then kept walking.

'Someone I should find.'

In his rush to distance himself from the conversation he had paced ahead of Helen. She ran to catch up.

'I don't know of any Clara,' she said. 'That is, if you wanted to know.'

'Thanks.'

The horses were waiting for them, stamping under their heavy burdens. Riding back to the Box-J, McDonough had little to say. Helen left him to his silence. A mile out of town a wave of sadness and grief washed over him. He had killed two men, hurt another, and was hated for something he'd had no hand in.

It was a strange fate that had guided him to this frozen mesa. In some ways he felt beholden to it. It had provided him with shelter and work and . . . His thoughts wandered to Adele. Fate had brought him to Adele, too, and for that he was grateful. Though they had talked only a few times he felt that he knew her, had known her all his life. There was something in her eyes when he looked at her. Not just desire or need, but hope rekindled. He felt it within himself, too.

He glanced over at Helen, so beautiful and strong-willed. What was it he saw in her eyes, he wondered. That she had feelings for him was undeniable. Why she did, he wasn't certain. They had barely had a complete conversation. There was so much she was responsible for maybe she didn't have the time to be subtle, to court. In many ways she was like a man, ruling with an iron hand, sure in her actions. That, too, was a powerful attraction, and even a little hypnotic. He had never met a woman like that.

Regardless of the women, his itch to travel was gone now. He had felt trapped when the trouble first began, unable to leave town because of the snow and the cold.

The itch to move on had been very strong then. But it had subsided as he grew more resentful toward those who heaped trouble on him. There was a terrible secret here on this mesa, the kind of thing that could tear a town apart. He didn't care much about the town, and apparently Gregory didn't deserve any posthumous kindness, but McDonough had suffered because of it. The thing had gotten under his skin and it rubbed raw like a saddle burr. He needed to see this finished.

They arrived at the Box-J early in the afternoon. Both Sven and Sarah came out to unload the horses, taking boxes and sacks and moving them inside. Without a word, McDonough and Helen separated. She went into the main house and he brought the horses into the barn where he stripped them of their saddles, brushed them, then turned each out into hay-filled stalls.

Sven came in, surly and grumbling under his breath. He dropped sacks of feed into a corner, making a sloppy job of it. With each trip he glanced over his shoulder at McDonough. On the fourth trip McDonough intercepted him, grabbing the youth by the front of his coat and shoving him up against a wall. So surprised was he by the violent action Sven couldn't strike back. He gasped in shock as his back slapped against the pine boards.

'Say it to my face,' McDonough told him.

Anger rising in him, Sven reached down and tried to break McDonough's hold. Fear coiled around his stomach when he couldn't budge the older man. McDonough's arms were like iron bars.

'I said you are here a few days and already t'row in jail.'

'And now I'm out again.'

Sven nodded as if McDonough's being released from jail confirmed his worst thoughts.

'Yah. And who got you out? Helen. You're anudder von, like Gregory. You'll try to drag her down, too.'

'Listen, kid, I get it. You're in love with Helen. You want to protect her. Well, forget it. You're out of your depth. She's too big for you.' Sven bristled at McDonough's words. He tried to push away from the wall but couldn't budge. 'You and me don't have to get along. It would be better if we did, but if not, well, that's fine with me, too. Just keep your mouth shut around me. Understand?'

Only after Sven nodded did McDonough release him.

'You're not so easy-going as you look,' Sven said.

'Not when I'm pushed, junior. Not when I'm pushed.'

They ate supper in silence and without Helen. Sarah served them but said nothing. She was like some wary mountain cat, uncertain what was going on but sure that there was danger in the air. After supper Sven left the cookhouse and went to bed.

'Here,' Sarah said, placing a full plate in front of McDonough.

'Your cooking is good, Sarah, but I've eaten my fill.'

She scowled. 'Take it to the main house.'

'I don't think so. I'd better get to the bunkhouse.'

'Uh-uh. After you bring this in.'

He got up and with resignation bowing his shoulders he took the plate of food up to the main house. He had never been inside so he wandered a bit, found a dining-room and a kitchen, both of them cold and unused. He passed through the kitchen and came to a large room with heavy furniture and an enormous fireplace along one wall. The fire burned dimly, adding a red glow to the room that brought out the earth-tones in the dark woods and uphol-stery. He was about to leave when he saw Helen's darkly golden hair glinting in the firelight. She was watching him, her face as solemn as stone.

'Sarah thought you could use some food,' he said. She didn't reply and for a long minute he stood there feeling stupid, waiting for her. At last he turned to leave but her voice stopped him.

'Put it here, Rafe,' she said, indicating a low table. 'Please.'

She sat in a high-backed chair upholstered in raw leather. McDonough set the plate down within her reach, nodded, and again turned to go.

'Rafe,' she said. 'I don't like this. Please, sit with me a moment.'

He felt his anger melting away but didn't understand how it had built up around him. Around the both of them. She had been upset with him at the jail. Jealous, really. But they had said nothing to each other to inflame the anger. The ride home had been silent. He hadn't really thought about it because he needed silence to do some thinking. He accepted that she had sensed his need and chose not to distract him. But when they had gotten back to the Box-J he saw that her dander was up and only now realized that the silence which had suited him so well had served only to irritate her. She had wanted to talk.

He sat opposite her on a thickly cushioned horsehair couch.

'When I was younger, Rafe, I saw my father do some hard things. Couldn't help but see it in an outfit small as ours. Afterward, he'd hold it all inside, not say a word. But I could see it was killing him. Sometimes, though, he would talk to me and it made him feel better.'

McDonough didn't answer right away. He didn't really want to talk to her about it.

'There's nothing to say, Helen,' he told her at last.

'Rafe, you killed two men.'

'They were trying to kill me.'

'That's a hard thing to say.'

'Dying's hard. I had no choice, Helen. They wanted me dead for no other reason than wearing another man's coat. They were foolish men who died like fools. I don't like that I had to do it, but I won't shy from owning to it.'

She was quiet for a moment, looking away from him into the fireplace and the embers dying there. Absently, he got up and began feeding the fire with more wood. Taking a poker he jabbed at the coals to spread the flame. The logs wouldn't ignite.

'If you're worried about what folks'll think of you . . .' he said.

'I'm not thinking about that.'

'. . . hiring a gunhand, and all,' he continued, 'I can leave.'

Helen slid out of the chair with an electric crackle, slipped up next to him and placed a gentle hand on his arm. He turned and bent his head toward her.

'I don't want you to go.' The meager firelight caught the blue of her eyes and lit them like smoldering coals. She pressed closer to him. 'I'm not Forester, Rafe. I don't need gun hands. But I do need a man who knows how to take care of himself. A man like that could name his price, on this ranch.'

'I've always taken care of myself,' he told her simply.

She smiled softly, lifting on her toes toward him.

'I know, Rafe,' she breathed.

Whether because of the fire or her nearness, McDonough's face burned and the heat made his eyes flicker and droop. He hung there for a moment, hovering above her, lips close, their breath on each other's cheeks.

90

Then he pulled away, quickly. Too quickly, for it brought a new fire to Helen's eyes, a steel hardness to her soft face. She turned from him and walked out of the room leaving him with a deep sense of foreboding in the pit of his stomach.

CHAPTER SEVEN

The next two days passed uneventfully. McDonough and Sven worked the cattle, rounding up the few that strayed from easy feed and water. Sven no longer acted surly or resentful. He had come to accept McDonough. The two men shared duties equally and worked well together. If Helen had noticed this change it did not register on her face. She was a stone to McDonough.

On the third day, McDonough announced he was going to track some strays that had wandered off toward the hills. He got up on Red, tossed a wave at Sven and rode off. Two miles from the ranch he stopped and dug into a snow-bank for a rucksack full of extra clothes and food he had secreted there the night before. There was a man in these hills somewhere, a man who knew Gregory, perhaps the man who had killed him. McDonough was going to find him, and it might take more than a day to do it.

Supplied, McDonough pointed Red west and south, aiming for the hills where he had seen the man and mule climbing. It had been only a glimpse, really, his mind more occupied that day with the approach of Forester's riders. But he had clearly seen a mule with something shiny flashing along its flank – probably a coffee-pot or a fry-pan – and a heavily bundled man leading it. If Forester was right – that Gregory had had a partner – then this was that man. Anyone else would be a fool to be out in such cold weather.

Cresting a hill, McDonough paused and looked back across the valley. It seemed to go on forever, as did the mountains behind him. Aspen grew here, leafless and shivering in the icy air, scrub brush, and tall, thin, blue spruce were bunched together in dense clumps beside the occasional black cottonwood below bare razorback ridges. The going was rough yet Red picked his way easily over the loose shale hidden beneath the snow. McDonough wondered at his own sanity; finding one man and a mule in such a wilderness was a foolish expectation.

McDonough paused and let Red paw at the new snow. He listened for sounds, sniffed the air for wood smoke, but there was nothing. He wondered, not for the first time, what a rustler would be doing in these hills. From what he had seen there were few places to hide cattle because the hills tended to fold in on one another, erasing even the hint of flat ground. There was no graze to be had, only hard climbing, trees, and rocks.

Skylined again, he looked back toward the valley, more distant now but clearly visible from this vantage. Against the vast, white backdrop he almost missed seeing the rider coming slowly from the east. He was but a black dot against the snow, yet unmistakable in the crystal-clear air. McDonough edged down the hill and into a clump of spruce to hide himself, making his movements slow and small. He couldn't tell if the rider had seen him before he disappeared behind one of the low hills.

McDonough waited, watching. The rider did not come back into view. Something made McDonough's back twitch and it put a buzzing in his ear. It was an old feeling, one that warned of trouble. Rarely did McDonough ride with his gun strapped to his hip, but he had belted it on the other day going to town and now wore it wherever he went. He dug under the heavy sheepskin coat, pulled out the Remington and broke open the cylinder to check its loads. Fumbling a little in the cold he slipped a sixth cartridge into the empty chamber directly beneath the hammer. He would trade caution for the extra firepower.

Reining his horse, he guided Red up and over the ragged hillcrest and down the other side. He found more of the same, another hill, this one more jagged than the last. Further east a bit were snow-dappled spires of rock and a wall etched and battered by ages of harsh weather. There were two low hills that folded in on each other and between them was where McDonough read his first sign.

It was a drop of blood.

Red snorted just once, catching the scent of the blood. He didn't shy, though, and allowed himself to be nudged closer to the glistening drop of red. McDonough dismounted, keeping back from the blood, which was fairly fresh, and looked about for other sign. Off to the right he saw the tracks – a man's and a pony's. Or perhaps a mule's. There was a smaller set, too, of deer, probably. It was hard to tell. The snow distorted the tracks. But they were fresh and headed into the narrow pass between the two low hills.

A man out hunting for meat, McDonough reasoned. Nothing much suspicious about that. Yet why come out so far into the hills, he wondered. Deer and elk came down to the valley in search of food. McDonough had seen them. A man could kill his fill and not have to wander so far from home. Unless the man wasn't wandering far because his home was in these hills.

94

Looking along the backtrail he saw the tracks rise up over a hill and around to the other side. McDonough could follow that trail and hope it led to something, or follow the fresh tracks and perhaps run into a man with a gun.

He mounted Red, reined over and set the horse to following the trail ahead. He found more blood, droplets at first and then small glistening puddles sitting on the icy snow. He crested the hill using a copse of thickly packed spruce to hide him. Below, he could see a narrow game trail cut through the trees to a small clearing. Smelling a strong scent of blood, he removed the Spencer from its boot and laid the heavy rifle across his saddle. Nothing moved in the hollow below.

In the clearing, McDonough found some animal viscera partly covered by snow. Among the jumble of tracks and bloody remains McDonough missed seeing the footprints leading up the rocks and back again. He did not know he had been observed, but he sensed eyes on him now.

The grizzled man calling himself Robaire lay hidden behind a rock above McDonough, a big Henry rifle gripped tightly in his mittened hands. Seeing McDonough's sheepskin coat and sombrero gave the man another start. Gregory was dead, he knew, and had left Robaire alone in the cold to find his own food. His beloved coffee was gone, the flour and sugar, too. If he hadn't found game he might have had to eat the blasted mule – and would still if the damned wolves found his kill. His other partner cared nothing for Robaire's privations, and this made him a bitter, angry man.

No, this wasn't Gregory come back to life. Gregory would not have to track him as this man was doing. Squinting against the snow glare, he suddenly recognized

McDonough as the rider from the other day – the one who had ridden off with Forester's men. A shiver of panic raced through him. He cocked the rifle and took aim.

Below, rifle in hand, McDonough followed the trail on foot, scanning the rocky walls around him. Something skittered above him. A puff of snow jumped off a ledge and glittered on the way down.

Suddenly a shot boomed in the close canyon and a chunk of snow exploded to McDonough's right. Already moving, he threw himself behind a boulder as another shot thumped into the ground where he had been standing.

He landed awkwardly, smacking his ribs on a hidden rock. Pain shooting through his side, McDonough rolled over and found himself wedged between two rocks. Another shot boomed and a chunk of the boulder shattered and sprayed shards and dust over him. McDonough lay still until the dust settled. He dared not look up over his protection, but from his vantage he could see Red back along the trail. The horse hadn't moved despite the thunderous gunshots and for once McDonough silently cursed the stout animal. It should have run. Instead it presented a big, tempting target to the shooter.

For long minutes McDonough lay in the snow, his ribcage burning and his legs freezing. He covered his mouth to dissipate the tell-tale steam of his breathing. He began to shiver. Eventually he called out.

'Hello! I mean you no harm,' McDonough yelled. Taking a deep breath was difficult and painful. No reply came. 'I just want to talk.'

'You will be dead,' a gravely voice eventually answered. 'Then you will do me no harm.'

McDonough recognized the accent as French Canadian.

'*J'suis ami,*' he called out.

The voice above him broke into uproarious laughter and when it died a rifle shot boomed and another part of McDonough's protective boulder shattered.

'I do not make friends with ghosts.'

'I'm no ghost.'

Another shot chipped away at the boulder and McDonough felt his stomach tighten at the thought of dying here in this lonely place. His thoughts turned to Adele, seeing her inviting face, smelling the aroma of baking bread around her. If he died, he wanted her to know. It was a simple and sudden need in him that was born whole in his mind. He wanted little else in life, but this was important to him.

After ten nerve-racking minutes of silence, McDonough shoved himself erect but before he could take another step his foot slipped on a hidden rock and he collapsed face down in the snow. He scrambled erect again, ran for the horse, grabbed its reins and pulled it behind him as he flew around the bend to safety. No shots had been fired; the Frenchman had fled.

Using the trees as cover, he began working his way over the hill, his eyes scanning ahead to every shadow. The going was slow and tedious but the trail was easy to spot. As he came down toward the trail again he saw more blood and viscera scattered on the snow. The man in the bearskin coat hadn't had time to clean out his kill before his tracks had been found, McDonough reasoned. Now each bloody blob pointed the way to his quarry.

Night was falling. His mind had been on the problem for the last hour, but he had seen no shelter. Tracking at night, no matter how easily followed was the trail, was dangerous business. Now that the sun was below the hills he turned in earnest to finding shelter. He had seen several rocky overhangs, but none of them would keep him out of the wind. At last he found a small cave, its horizontal mouth a slit in the rock. He crawled in and found a compact but relatively dry room, shallow with no signs of habitation.

Below the cave was a deep alcove that the wind didn't touch. He led Red to this and tied him loosely to a tree. From the meager supplies tied to his saddle, he brought out a small bag of oats and fed this to the animal.

'Sorry about the accommodations, friend,' he said, patting the horse. 'Mine won't be much better.' He left the saddle on, loosened a little at the cinch.

In the tiny cave, McDonough lit a fire and sucked on raw coffee beans all night to help keep himself awake, the Spencer and Remington close at hand. By morning his stomach was churning sourly. He felt haggard and worn.

He came out of the cave, then stopped short. There was blood on the snow and small blobs of entrails which hadn't been there the night before.

McDonough backed up against the rock, shifting the weight of his kit so he could better balance the rifle. Scanning intensely, he swept his eyes over every rock and tree in view.

Carefully, he edged his way down to the hollow where Red had spent the night. The horse snorted an impatient greeting.

'Easy, fella.'

A sound came up with the wind so low that it was almost beyond his hearing. But Red heard it and he stamped nervously.

'Yeah, I hear it, too,' he told the animal in gentle tones as he tied his kit behind the highbacked saddle.

Rather than ride, McDonough led the horse back onto the trail, around the viscera, and over the hill. The man in the bearskins, he now realized, had been leaving a deliberate trail, one designed to draw McDonough to him and to attract others as well.

A flash of movement caught the edge of McDonough's sight. He whirled about. It was gone. The crack of a branch from behind made Red toss his head. The low, constant sound seemed to breathe with the wind.

The tracks were still clear. No new snow had fallen. In fact the wind had turned, coming now from the south and bringing with it warmer air. The hills should have started to come to life again with animal sounds and movements, but all was deathly still.

Coming over a rise McDonough saw a bowl below him ringed by trees and sharply etched peaks. He pulled Red off the trail and scanned the rocks, but saw nothing. The trail led down into the rounded hollow. It was a trap, McDonough could see that right off. A double-edged one, too, if he was any judge of nature's sounds.

The background noise had grown into a low, deep rumble. It came from all around. He could see movement again in the trees. A flash of gray, a bit of brown. Streaks that darted from tree to rock.

He turned again to the trail. In a straight line it swooped down off the hill and then back up the other side of the bowl. At the bottom, there were more bits of red. Bait for the trap. The trail disappeared through a narrow passage on the far side, its rocky prominences overlooking the bowl like sentries. There, the man in the bearskins would be waiting with his rifle trained on the trail.

McDonough hopped onto Red. 'Don't have much of a choice, fella,' he said. 'We'll make a run for it.' He pulled the Spencer out of its boot and laid it across the saddle.

Crying out a war whoop, McDonough spurred the roan forward and they shot down off the hill kicking up great puffs of snow. Instantly, the low rumbling sound became excited barks and growls. Half a dozen wolves appeared suddenly and sped off in pursuit.

McDonough gained the bottom of the bowl and veered around the bloody bait. The quick movement saved him as a gout of snow spurted into the air, followed immediately by the echoing crack of a rifle.

Yanking Red's reins over, McDonough changed course abruptly. The angry buzz of another rifle bullet zipped past McDonough's ear. The quick yelp from a wolf told him just how close behind him was the ravenous pack.

Red's momentum carried them part-way up the hill until slippery rock and thick snowdrifts began to slow the animal. Now sudden movement was impossible. McDonough fired from the saddle, wild shots that cracked off the rock above. The man in the bearskins fired several more shots into the snow in front of Red. The horse shied, its nerve shattering.

Suddenly the horse slipped and tumbled. McDonough threw himself from the saddle and landed on his back, snow cushioning his fall.

Further down the hill, the wolves stopped. Spread out in a wide arc around him, the five remaining beasts snarled wetly, baring teeth and barking with bloodlust. For a long moment they stood rooted in place, then the large gray one took a step forward and they all charged.

The Remington buried under his coat, McDonough had only the twelve shots in his Spencer. From his seat in the snow, he leveled the weapon at the gray wolf leader and fired. The cagey beast sensed the attack and dodged.

McDonough missed.

He swung the rifle and fired three quick shots. One of the attacking wolves was felled. Another circled around toward Red. The horse was behind McDonough and up the hill, fighting against a snowdrift. Panic was taking him over, driving him to frenzied flight.

The third wolf snarled, saliva oozing from its bared snout. Its eyes were alive with a haunting red glow. Before McDonough could swing the rifle back on target, the creature leapt. Their bodies crashed together, the beast's fangs sinking deep into his heavy sheepskin coat, jaws tightening on McDonough's forearm. Searing pain shot through his arm. Frantically he beat the animal with his rifle butt until it let go his arm, snarling viciously as it backed away, snapping at the weapon.

McDonough fired and the sound briefly startled the wolf. It paused and took a half-step back. Slicing with a powerful backhand, McDonough swung the Spencer's barrel against the animal. The wolf yelped and stumbled, a blot of red erupting on its head. Then McDonough fired point blank and the animal dropped soundlessly to the snow.

A quick glance over his shoulder showed McDonough that Red was still fending off one of the beasts. Then a low growl snapped McDonough's attention back to the gray leader. He turned just in time to see the wolf jump, teeth bared. McDonough lifted the Spencer in front of him, hands at either end of the rifle, and caught the animal's jaws on the long barrel. Instantly he was on his feet and pushing the wolf backwards downhill, not allowing the beast to free its salivating mouth.

The wolf stumbled and fell away, its mouth suddenly free. It rolled downhill, scrambling to right itself. For an instant it paused, gulping air, then, growling angrily, it leapt in for the kill. McDonough dropped the muzzle on target and levered two quick shots. The impact made the wolf convulse in mid-air and drop in a heap to the snow.

McDonough turned uphill and watched the lone remaining wolf move uncertainly away from Red. Snarling, the creature backed down the hill then up the other side, always keeping its quarry in sight. The snarls became more defiant as McDonough leveled the rifle and fired, killing the animal.

His hands shaking, McDonough ran to the roan and dug into the saddlebags for more cartridges. He kept a watchful eye on the spires at the top of the bowl as he reloaded. As he turned Red uphill, two shots boomed in the small hollow. Snow spurted into the air ten feet from him.

McDonough dropped to the snow, slid beneath Red's legs and began firing up at the spires. Rock shattered violently. The echoing gunshots made it sound as if a cavalry volley had been loosed in the tiny bowl. Red screamed but did not move.

His rifle empty, McDonough crawled out from under the horse, fished out more cartridges, and reloaded. Then he drove Red up the hill ahead of him, rifle ready, eyes scouring the rocks above him. He saw no sign of the shooter, only spent brass and tracks leading away.

Trembling, his arm throbbing, McDonough decided not to follow immediately. Despite the cold he shucked his coat and the denim jacket underneath to examine his arm. The wolf's fangs had cut through the clothing down to his shirt. The heavy cotton cloth was punctured and as he rolled up the sleeve he could see deep teeth marks on his arm, even now purpling with bruising. But the skin had only been scraped, not broken.

He snatched a handful of snow, pressed it against his arm and held it there for several minutes until the area numbed. Then he brushed the snow away, buttoned his sleeve and got dressed. The damage wasn't too bad.

Red tossed his head and snorted.

'You shaky, too, huh?' McDonough asked with a chuckle. He went over to the roan and ran a hand along the horse's legs. There were no bite-marks or blood. 'Looks like we got away lucky, fella.'

Leading the horse, McDonough followed the tracks of the man in the bearskin coat. Down the hill, into the thicket of trees they went, but when they came to a clearing, the tracks were gone. Here, windblown rocky peaks only lightly dusted with snow jutted up off the clearing floor. Narrow passes cut through these rugged hills and thin game trails clung to the rock, offering dozens of ways for a man to hide or escape. For an hour McDonough searched among the rocks but could not pick up the man's tracks again.

He turned and paused. Something reflected dully in the corner of his eye. He bent and saw a piece of canvas, smaller than his palm, with its edges torn as if the piece it came from had ripped on the barbed rocks. Beside it was a stone, unnaturally jagged. Someone had used a pick to pry it loose from its home. The stone was gray and black and wound through it were thick streaks of something flat and sallow.

McDonough pocketed the stone, climbed aboard Red and turned the horse north. They came down out of the hills around midday, into the great, endless valley miles east of Helen's Box-J ranch. He let the horse rest for a few moments, uncertain what he should do. He knew that

Helen would be angry with him for leaving suddenly. Angry enough to fire him if he stayed away too long. He could go back to her now and tell her he had been chasing down strays. It was a thin lie, but she wouldn't question it.

But he also felt a powerful drive to uncover the dirty truth this valley was hiding. He owed nothing to the dead man, Gregory, and he was no lawman. Still, there was the woman Clara. He owed her nothing, either, yet he imagined her alone, waiting, hoping for word that would never come. Something about that loneliness knotted his stomach. He couldn't ignore that feeling. Climbing aboard Red, McDonough decided he would ride to town and report what he had found to Constable Thackery. If the delay cost him his job, so be it.

As he crossed the valley toward Sprigensguth he wondered idly about Gregory's killer. Almost everyone he'd met had a reason to kill him: the man in the bearskin coat, Danvers and his crowd in town, Forester and his foreman Gibson, and even Sven. He thought of the Swedish boy, foolishly in love with Helen, a woman too big for him to handle, and could see him giving Gregory that beating. But the boy carried a large-caliber gun. In fact, everyone he met seemed to carry a large-caliber gun. Sven might have beaten Gregory to death but he wouldn't have shot him and left him to die.

Sometime later, unseen by McDonough, another set of tracks crossed his. They were the tracks of a man leading mule.

Sprigensguth was dark when McDonough arrived. The café was closed. Passing it he felt a pang in his chest. It hadn't been long since he had last seen Adele, yet it felt like months. He turned down Butte Street, stopping at the jail. He had just tied the roan to the hitching rail when the door opened and Constable Thackery stepped outside. McDonough's rough, bearded face fell into the light of a lantern and made the constable jump.

'McDonough! You startled me.'

'You're leaving?'

'Well, hell, man, I don't live here. Every once in a while I go home to sleep.'

'Let's go back inside and talk. You got coffee?'

Thackery shrugged under his thick coat and opened the door. After lighting lanterns and seeing to the fire and coffee, the constable sat behind his desk and waved McDonough to a chair. With a cup of coffee in his frozen hands, McDonough told of his adventures in the hills south of town.

'You think this fella in the bearhide is Gregory's partner.'

McDonough shrugged. 'Don't know. But if he knew Gregory I have questions to ask.'

'About this Clara,' Thackery said.

'Yeah. Look, Forester believes Gregory had a partner and that the man was hiding out in the hills. Maybe it wasn't this hermit but it's worth finding out.'

'I'll get word to Forester, then.'

'You can't. He'll kill him.'

Thackery scowled. 'You want me to go after him, don't you?'

'I could file a complaint, if that would help.'

Thackery pushed his coffee away with disgust.

'Well, I sure ain't going out there until morning.'

'I don't expect either of us will,' McDonough said, grinning. 'There's something else.' He rose to his feet, took the stone from his pocket and dropped it onto the desk.

Thackery examined it, his face falling with disappointment.

'Gold,' he said, quietly.

'Looks that way to me. And if I've got the lay of the territory right, it was dug up on Forester land.'

'Yeah, well, according to you, your sense of direction isn't very good.' Thackery sighed heavily. 'Forester'll kill him for sure.' The constable stood and began putting out the lanterns and dampening the stove fire. 'Meet me tomorrow morning. Not too early, mind you. We'll get breakfast and see about finding this man in the bearhide coat.'

McDonough declined an invitation to dinner, preferring to get his horse stabled and then put himself to bed at the hotel. But after he had wakened the trembling Jaynes at the livery stable, McDonough felt restless. For a long moment he stared down the street toward the darkened café windows, then he turned away from the hotel. At the end of the street he passed the café and kept walking in the dark toward a small brick house belching smoke from a fat chimney. There was an iron gate around the yard, packed now with snowdrift, and inside were the outlines of planter boxes. A small section of the yard was fenced with wire and the thin remains of latticework tilted in one corner. The house was neat and trim, well kept. A warm, golden light emanated from the curtained front window.

He hesitated for a moment after passing through the open gate. It was late. She might be asleep. When he knocked he did so lightly, half-afraid she would come to the door. After a bit, a light waggled behind the thin curtains, which parted slightly to reveal briefly a dark face.

A moment later, the door snapped open.

'Rafe, come in. Hurry,' Adele said, wrapped yet shivering in a thick robe.

McDonough stamped his feet then hurried across the threshold. Adele came to him and began helping him out of his coat.

'Take these off and warm up by the fire. Whatever are you doing out tonight?'

She didn't wait for an answer. She took the rifle and saddle bags he had brought with him from the livery barn and set them by the door. His coat she hooked over a wooden chair by the hearth in the next room.

'Sit here,' she told him, offering an upholstered chair. She worked it closer to the fireplace, then raked the coals with a poker and added two pieces of wood. 'I'll get you some coffee.'

'Don't go to any trouble, Adele,' he told her, but she was already gone, down a short hallway where a light suddenly came to life.

'Sit, Rafe. It's no trouble.'

So, he sat. The flames began to waken, crackling again to life, snapping as if annoyed to be put back into service. McDonough settled into the chair's thick cushions and enjoyed the quiet symphony of the fire. He was warming, even down deep, and he felt peacefulness infuse his body. Even the throbbing in his arm had stopped. So long in the saddle, so far from where he had begun, it was nice to stop and rest and be with someone, if only for a little while.

Outside, Robaire watched as McDonough disappeared into the warm, inviting house, anger and jealousy filling him. In the dark he patted his coat, feeling the thick, small sacks tied about his belt-loops and suspenders. He had worked hard for many months, hungry, alone, and for what? To give up most of what he mined to his partners? Murder entered Robaire's thoughts. He would give up none of his gold, and the thought of keeping all of his bounty warmed him. He'd have to kill this stranger, too, but no matter. It would be worth it.

Suddenly, from the shadows, a hand grabbed him and slammed him against a wall, then dragged him like an old rag-doll into a blackened alley.

'What are you doing here?' a muffled, gravely voice demanded.

Shaking, the Frenchman asked: 'Who are you?'

'You know who I am.'

It was too dark in the alley to see, yet Robaire squinted and craned his neck forward. Yes, Robaire thought, I do know you.

'Answer me,' the man in the shadows commanded.

'There was a feller up in the hills tracking me. He is trouble, for all of us.'

Robaire felt the man's grip loosen.

'The man in the street just now?'

'That's him. He knows something.'

'McDonough.' The man spat the name as if it were poison.

'McDonough, eh? Well, *monsieur* McDonough is clever and deadly. He was very close to the mine.'

'Fool!' Robaire's head jerked as a hand smashed against his temple. 'I told you to stay under cover.'

'I must eat!'

Robaire had been snaking his hand inside his coat and now felt the worn, aged butt of his gun. He called it a blunderbuss for its size and booming sound. It would make a big hole, too, especially fired at such close range. The sound of a cocking revolver and the press of a muzzle against his chest stayed his hand.

'You'll eat lead, you fat, smelly pig.' To Robaire the man sounded almost drunk. His words seemed to slosh around in his mouth.

'*Monsieur*, we are partners, *oui?*' the Frenchman said, trembling. 'You, me, and . . .' he let the sentence hang in the air, unfinished.

Another pause. The blackness began working on Robaire's nerves. He preferred being able to see his enemy.

'So you followed him,' the man said, finally.

'*Oui.* To kill him.'

The man took hold of Robaire's arm, pulled him out of the alley and steered him away from Adele's house. Light fell on the pair and, with scheming eyes, the Frenchman looked up at his companion. Rubbing his inflamed, crooked jaw Strap Gibson said:

'No. I kill him. McDonough is mine.'

CHAPTER EIGHT

She hadn't wanted to waken him but when she set the tray of coffee and cups down on the table the tinkling sound it made stirred him.

'Adele,' he said, looking nervously toward the night-shrouded window. 'How long have I been out.'

'A few minutes.'

Sitting forward McDonough rubbed his eyes and face, trying to bring them back to life.

'You're tired.'

'Yes,' he said with a short nod. 'I am tired.' He looked up at her, the warm glow of the fire casting a soft haze around her. She had changed while he slept. The robe was gone and she wore a thick, velvety green dress with a modest neckline, simple yet beautiful. It shimmered in the firelight. Under his gaze she shifted a little. He felt too aware of staring at her, suddenly, and turned away.

'We didn't get to have that coffee,' she said, starting to pour.

'Could use that.' He took the cup and found himself staring at her again. Helen might be prettier, McDonough thought, but he had never seen a more beautiful woman than Adele. He caught himself smiling and glanced away.

'I like that,' she told him. 'You have a nice smile.'

On the tray beside the coffee-pot were two plates with thick slices of dried apple and cherry pie. Seeing the plates his stomach growled loudly.

Adele laughed. 'Well, take one, Rafe. I brought them for you.'

'You don't have to . . .'

'Oh, just eat the pie.'

So he did, wiping both plates clean with the crust.

'I do thank you. Hadn't eaten for much of the day. And your café was closed when I got to town.'

'You didn't want to go rustle up a sandwich at one of the saloons?'

'Never crossed my mind.'

He wasn't sure but as Adele gathered the plates and stacked them neatly on the tray he thought he saw her blush.

'I hear Sarah is a good cook for Helen.'

'Passable.' Adele smiled now as she poured more coffee. 'Adele, I'm sorry to have wakened you.' He sat at the edge of the chair, his hands fidgeting with his coffee cup.

'I'm glad you came, Rafe.'

For a few minutes they sat and watched the fire.

'I've been thinking about you, Adele. Nights get kind of lonely at the ranch.'

A teasing smile played on her lips.

'You've got Sven in the bunkhouse,' she suggested. 'You can play cards.'

'Nah. He goes to sleep quick and is out like a baby.'

'What have you been thinking about me, Rafe?'

'That I like it when I'm around you. That, after this mess is figured out, I'd want to stay and have a steady diet of that pie.'

Her face curled up, but not unpleasantly.

'Men and pie. Is that all you think about, Rafe? Food?'

'No, ma'am. Not all.'

Now he was certain she was blushing for she stood suddenly and moved toward the fireplace, keeping her back to him. The green of her dress caught the firelight like some mystical lantern radiating an ethereal luminescence. He wanted to stand up and go to her but couldn't muster the courage. Somehow, the women he had known before were different. He had understood what to do with them.

'Did you have any luck finding Clara?'

'No. She's still a mystery.'

Adele took something from the fireplace overmantle and held it out for him. It was a piece of paper and a pencil.

'Still no envelopes, but you'll need these to write her when you find out who she is.'

He rose and went to Adele, standing only inches from her. He took the paper and pencil and smiled his thanks. She smiled, too, almost laughing at how unsure he seemed. Then he leaned down and kissed her with soft, tentative lips. He was starting to straighten when Adele slipped a hand around his neck and pulled him down and kissed him again.

'I shouldn't stay,' he whispered, gently pushing away.

'You just got here.' There was a sparkle of fear in her eyes. He moved toward her again and kissed her. He would be back, and now she realized it, too.

'The constable and I have an early morning tomorrow,' he said, then told her of the man in the bearhide coat hiding in the hills.

'You don't know who he is?'

'No. But he's afraid of being seen.'

'Why, Rafe? Why would he be?'

He took the stone from his pocket and handed it Adele. She needed only a glance to know what it was. A sad smile crossed her lips and she shook her head.

'Got a similar response from Thackery when I showed him that rock.'

'Gold,' she said. 'Another boom.'

'Maybe.'

Adele stepped away from the fire and sat.

'No maybes about it, Rafe. I've seen it often enough. Word will get out and come spring there'll be hundreds, maybe thousands of people combing these hills for mines and panning the streams.' She tossed the gold-flecked rock in her hand. 'I'm not from Sprigensguth, Rafe. I came here with a gold-rush.'

He laughed. 'You were a miner?'

'No. I was coming west to San Francisco when our stage was robbed and I was left penniless. I worked in shops and restaurants just to get by. Then I got caught in a boom-town and made some good money. I followed to the next boomtown and opened my own café. Rafe, the money I made was obscene, even charging fair prices.'

'Why didn't you go on to San Francisco then?'

'Well, I got to Sprigensguth just as it boomed. The hills played out quickly, though, and everyone moved on. Everyone but me. Rafe, it's cold and desolate-looking now with nothing but endless tracts of snow. But the rest of the year – oh, and especially in the spring, Rafe – it's so beau-tiful it takes my breath away. I couldn't leave it now for all the gold there is.' She looked off into the fire, her eyes misty with a far away gaze. 'I guess I was looking for some-thing, Rafe. Didn't know it, but I was.'

'You found it here.'

Smiling at him she said: 'Yes. At least some of it. I – I've been waiting for the rest for a long time now.'

He sat beside her and kissed her slowly.

'It is good land,' he said. 'And you think a boom will ruin it, don't you?'

'A boomtown is an ugly thing. It brings a lot of trouble. Sprigensguth serves a purpose out here for all of the ranchers. It's a good town. But a gold rush could destroy it.'

'There might not be much gold,' he suggested weakly.

'It doesn't take much, Rafe. Not much at all.'

He lifted Adele to her feet and wrapped his arms around her to soothe her, surprised at how much comfort he took in their embrace. Easing away from him she looked up and smiled.

'I thought you were going.'

'I am. But not far, and not for long.'

'I know.'

He kissed her again at the door, desperate to get out and let the cold air clear his head. The feeling he had with Adele was something he had never imagined. The other women he had known were so different. No, he realized, it wasn't the women who were different. He was. He had changed.

Wrapped in the warm sheepskin coat, sombrero shoved down on his head, McDonough made his way back to the hotel. He'd probably have to wake the surly desk clerk, demand a room. He thought of the small stove in the hotel room, the meager fire that it held, and paused to glance back at Adele's house. The fire was pleasanter there than any place he had ever been. He let out a long sigh that turned to a shiver and continued walking.

'Out for a stroll?'

The voice had come from the shadows beneath a wooden awning. McDonough spun to face it, lifting the rifle and dropping his saddle bags.

'Whoa, pardner! Don't shoot the law.'

Nels Thackery stepped out into the street, grinning.

'Glad you came out when you did. Getting a mite chilly for standing around.'

Suspicion curdled McDonough's face.

'Why were you hiding out here?'

'Not really hiding. Just waiting. Figured after your last visit to town it might be prudent to see you safely home.'

'Straight to the hotel, Constable. No saloons for me tonight.'

'Glad to hear it.' Tossing a glance down the street he added: 'She's a fine woman, that Adele.'

'Yes, she is.'

'A good woman, too.'

'Better'n a forty-a-month ranny deserves.'

Thackery nodded. 'Maybe. Then again, maybe not. Come on. Let's get you to the hotel.'

The two had walked a few paces when McDonough turned and asked:

'How'd you know where I was?'

'Just a guess,' Thackery chuckled. 'Just a guess.'

He didn't know what it was that had stirred him but he became instantly awake. For a moment his mind reeled as if he were dizzy, looking around for something familiar. He was in a hotel room, he reminded himself, and saw the black stove in the corner, dying coals peaking out through the grating like devil eyes. He had been asleep for perhaps two hours.

The room was dark and the chill, which had never been vanquished fully by the weak embers, had tightened its icy grasp. Pale moonlight was making shadowy crosses on the paper window-shades. A sliver of yellow light peered under the door. Nothing was moving outside. Yet the quiet of it all unnerved him, for something had disturbed his subconscious.

Slipping his revolver out of its leather, McDonough climbed out of bed and pressed himself into a corner. He fought with his lungs to control his breathing, calm his nerves. Anger began growing in him. He had always avoided trouble, keeping the credo that life was too short to fight over another man's problems. But here trouble had found him, and all of it over a dead man's hat. The thought infuriated him.

McDonough cocked the gun and waited. Soon, a wavering shadow fell onto the window shade.

The window creaked once as it opened and McDonough heard a sharp gasp from someone outside. A stream of cold air shot across the room. Quickly, McDonough grabbed the chair and shoved it up under the doorknob, his movements covered by the actions of the man outside.

The window fully open now, the shade lifted as a leg pushed inside and dropped to the floor. McDonough lunged out and punched through the paper shade. His fingers fell onto a heavy coat, which he grabbed by the handful and yanked. A body flew into the room and landed on the floor with a grunt, the spur of one boot snagging on the sill. There was barely enough light to make out a bearded face and dark, close-set eyes.

Shock had frozen the man but he recovered quickly, bringing up an arm, the end of it showing a steely glint.

McDonough fired twice and the man thumped back against the wooden floor with a wheezing gasp and died.

Another shot, from outside, shattered window glass and McDonough felt a tug at his arm. He spun to the floor, firing wildly out the window. The stove clanged loudly on the heels of another gunshot as McDonough scrambled to get away from the broken glass. He cursed silently. Two bullets left and his cartridge belt was across the room.

The unseen gunman fired again, the bullet slapping into the mattress. McDonough was about to return fire when he heard the muffled sound of someone running away.

His hand shaking, McDonough darted across the room and scooped up his gun belt. He reloaded quickly, then stamped into his boots, grabbed his coat, and climbed out the smashed window. Anger was heavy in him now.

Despite the gunshots, the street was quiet, empty. McDonough saw the footprints immediately and followed them to a dark corner. Here there were two deeper prints and several other lighter ones. Three cigarette butts had been extinguished in the snow. It was here that the one gunman had waited until the first man had made his fatal move.

A shadow crossed the street to the north of town and McDonough, caught in the open, tensed, waiting for a bullet that didn't come. Keeping under cover as much as possible, McDonough followed.

Slightly north of town the street broke up and the neat rows of buildings ended. Beyond were several houses and sheds, each turned to face a different direction. The shooter wouldn't leave town, couldn't, for beyond the hodge-podge of ramshackle buildings was nothing but frozen prairie.

About thirty feet away was a shack that was dark and looked abandoned. Steeling himself, McDonough kicked off the boardwalk and ran for it. He tripped a few yards from the shack, tumbling and rolling in the snow. Scrambling to his feet, he fell against the shack wall, pressing his back against the cracked and rotting wood. The cold was getting to him now, stiffening his fingers. He was breathing too hard, he knew, and tried to calm himself. Cautiously, he peeked around the corner. No one was there.

Stepping with care he slid along the weather-beaten wood to the next corner. Again, no one was waiting for him.

The pale half-moon reflected off the snow, giving the landscape an eerie glow. It was enough light by which to make out shapes, but not much more. McDonough could see a tiny house, lit from within and casting jaundiced squares of light onto the snow. Smoke belched from a narrow brick chimney. Behind it was another shack, and further out was another. Squinting, McDonough peered at the far structure. Something had moved there.

Suddenly a shot flashed in the dark and a bullet spat off the cracked wood next to McDonough's right ear. He threw himself to the ground and rolled behind an abandoned barrel. Then he jumped to his feet and ran for the tiny house. He stumbled again and slammed against the house's stone base. For a moment he lay there out of the line of fire, dazed, exhausted, and cold.

The shooter was trapped now. There were no more places to hide after that far shack. He'd have to double back. McDonough rose off the frozen ground and began making his way forward.

Still, there was silence. He half-expected to hear the

118

other man's breathing or the swishing sound of boots running through snow. McDonough winced with each step he took for, to his ears, it sounded like thunder when his boot crunched down on snow. The shooter must be not moving, he thought; he's waiting for me.

Carefully McDonough worked his way around the corner of the house, heading away from the shack, which was now out of his vision. If he could circle around and surprise the shooter he might be able to take the man alive.

Ducking around the far corner of the house he again sighted the shack, dark and dead against the moonlit snow. No movement, no sounds. The gunman could have gotten away as McDonough circled the house, but he didn't think so. That meant he had to be inside or behind the shack. Either way, it was foolhardy to approach.

McDonough leveled the Remington, and fired two quick shots into the shack.

'I can keep this up all night,' he called.

No one answered. Then a shot low to the ground blasted out from inside the shack. McDonough returned fire and saw something fall with a muffled thump. Running forward he charged into the shed and fell onto the thing that had tipped over. Immediately he knew he had been tricked. He had dropped onto a rake that had been wrapped in burlap sacks.

Several shots slapped against the aged wood. McDonough rolled back out of the light, then watched as the door slammed shut with a heavy thud, trapping him inside. Two more shots splintered holes in the pine-board walls, forcing McDonough to the ground.

He slithered into a corner, keeping low, expecting more bullets. But they didn't come. Instead, silence pressed down on him like an anvil. He dared not move for fear of making a noise. His anger was at a fever pitch, but now directed inward. He had fallen for the trap like a tenderfoot.

A blast sent a shudder through the shack and in the next second jets of flame burst skyward outside, visible through the cracks in the plank walls. McDonough jumped to his feet just as two bullets smashed into the room. He dropped again, waited, then rose and swiftly ran to the door. Locked, barred somehow from the outside.

He pounded on the door, yelling for help. Already smoke had begun seeping into the room as flames licked the air between the boards. Putting his shoulder to the door, he gave a mighty shove, but the thing wouldn't budge. Panic rising, he ran at it, crushing his shoulder against the unforgiving wood.

Flames began eating at the wood, dry and dead as tinder, sparks snapping at him like fireworks. The roof had caught fire and three walls were engulfed. The roar of it was deafening.

Taking his revolver, McDonough brought his muzzle close to the burning wood and fired. A hole half the size of his fist opened in the wall. Methodically he worked his way up the wall, shooting holes in the planks. His eyes watered from the heat and smoke and his fingers burned as the gun became unbearably hot. Each shot echoed in the close room like cannon fire until his ears throbbed with pain. He had put sixteen holes in the wood before he ran out of bullets.

Staggering back a step, he lifted his boot and kicked at the broken wall. It cracked and sprayed brittle sparks over his trousers. He kicked again and his pant-leg caught fire. A third kick sent a small circle of burning wood sizzling off into the night. The hole it created was barely large enough for McDonough's shoulders. He dived for the opening, squeezed himself out of the shack and landed in a muddy puddle of melted snow. Coughing, gagging, he rolled in a snow-bank as he slapped at his coat and pants to put out the several small fires that had erupted on his clothing.

Lanterns wobbled in the distance. He could hear the sound of people running, confused voices calling out. One lantern pushed through a small crowd that had gathered a safe distance from the fire. As the lantern light neared, McDonough could make out the features of Constable Thackery.

The bearded policeman looked down at McDonough, then over at the shack, just now collapsing. A shower of sparks jetted up into the night sky. Glancing at the front of the crumbling shack, McDonough could see a barrel wedged up against the door. It had caught fire, too, the wood dissolving and the iron bands melting in the intense heat.

McDonough got to his feet slowly, his breath ragged and his hands shaking. The revolver in his right fist seemed grafted to his skin. It wasn't until he pushed it into his holster that he could pry his fingers from the butt. Quickly, he outlined for the constable the deadly events of the past half-hour, including the corpse in his room and the mystery gunman.

'You are a troublesome sort.' Thackery's displeasure was plain on his hard-set face. But something softened in his eyes suddenly and he shrugged. 'Guess it's better I don't have to clean up your corpse,' he said.

'I will agree with you there.'

Thackery turned to several of the townspeople and waved them forward. He instructed them to put out the fire, then told another to get the town doctor.

'He fills in as coroner,' Thackery explained.

'Comforting.'

'I'll be a bit, McDonough. Why don't you go gather up your things. You're staying with me tonight. I don't want any more of these incidents, and it looks like you could use a nanny.'

'Yeah,' McDonough agreed. 'Preferably one toting a Colt revolver.'

Next morning, with the weather warming, the Plains Café was busy for breakfast. The murmur and buzz of dozens of customers could be heard even before McDonough and Thackery opened the door to enter. They found a table in the corner, sat, and waited until coffee was poured before speaking.

'You boys don't look so good,' Adele said. 'Maybe I'd better leave the pot.'

Each man wore a haggard expression; neither had shaved. Their bodies seemed to slump inside their clothing.

'Maybe you'd better,' McDonough said, mustering a smile for Adele. His eyes were the only bright things about him this morning, and only when he looked at Adele.

She smiled, too, finding it hard to look away from him.

'I understand you had some trouble last night, Nels. Some shooting.'

Thackery tossed a tired head at McDonough.

'His trouble. I came in at the end.'

An electric shock passed through her and she knelt beside McDonough, putting a hand to his arm.

'Rafe, are you . . . ?'

'I'm fine,' he said. His hand was on her shoulder, rubbing gently. He wanted to pull her close and kiss her. 'There's a shed at the end of Butte Street that didn't make it, though.'

'And a dead man in our boy's hotel room,' Thackery added sourly.

'Rafe!'

'It's oke.' He smiled weakly, enough to reassure her.

'Who was it?' she asked.

'Ted Eberwein,' Thackery told her. She shrugged and shook her head. 'You wouldn't know him, probably. One of the town toughs. Always suspected him of having robbed the Lavina stage a few months back, but the witnesses weren't much help identifying him. He hung out at Danvers' most days. Most nights, too.'

'It's that damned hat, Rafe,' she cursed, her eyes starting to glisten.

'No, Adele. It's not that. Not any more.'

Blast, he didn't care how many people saw. McDonough pulled Adele toward him, gently lifting her, and kissed her. Adele melted into him, then stiffened a little and stood. She swept the front of her brown gingham dress with propriety, pressing the bright yellow apron with the flat of her hand.

'I'll put some breakfast together for you boys that'll get you up and going. I'll be right back.' Leaving the coffee-pot, she twirled and hurried to the kitchen.

Pouring more coffee into his cup Thackery said:

'Reverend's gonna have you both in church twice on Sundays if you keep that up.'

'Yes, Rafe, it was quite unseemly,' Helen said, stepping up to their table. Her face was a tight mask but anger lay just beneath the surface. It bubbled up through her eyes and stabbed at him. 'When I hire a man, he usually stays around the ranch to do his work.'

Thackery stood and offered his chair but Helen didn't budge, didn't even acknowledge the constable.

'I ran into some trouble and came to tell the law.' McDonough chose his words carefully, feeling his throat tighten as he spoke. He threw a quick glance toward the kitchen and saw Adele at the order window, watching him.

'If it's trouble on my range, you come tell me first,' she demanded. She had removed her low-crowned hat and held it in tight, clenched fists. Her sleek hair fell across one eye as she spoke and she let it stay there half-covering her face.

'It wasn't,' he told her.

Helen laughed with a disdainful huff.

'You don't like breakfast at the ranch any more? You had kind words for Sarah's cooking.'

'She's just fine, Helen.'

'Only this is better, right?'

'I'll be back in a day or two. The constable and I have . . . something to do.'

'No you don't, Rafe. I hired you. You're mine. I need you back at the ranch. We'll let the law handle its own business.'

The murmur of the crowd had died down and necks were craned in their direction.

'Sit down, Helen,' McDonough said, conscious of the prying eyes on him. 'Let's talk quietly.'

'No. Get your things.'

McDonough reached for the coffee-pot with deliberate motion and poured himself another cup. Then he slowly began sipping at it.

Helen shook with impotent rage. If she were a man,

McDonough thought, she would have punched him. Instead she reached into her coat pocket, drew out two heavy coins and tossed them on the table. They were double eagles.

'Your time,' she said. 'Though you ain't been worth even half that.' She fitted the hat carefully back onto her head. 'Don't bother to come back to the Box-J. I don't figure there's anything you want back at the ranch.'

'I've got a horse,' he said.

Helen's right hand jerked toward her coat pocket and for an instant McDonough wondered if she would draw on him. She was a fiery woman, quick-tempered and determined to get what she wanted. In just a short time with her he had seen that clearly. Now he wondered if she would kill to get what she wanted.

'I'll have Sven bring it to town. Goodbye, Rafe.'

Stiff as a board, she turned and strode from the restaurant. Thackery took his seat, slumping with relief.

'That's some woman.'

'You're welcome to her.'

The constable shook his head.

'No thank you.' Then he laughed and lightly punched McDonough's arm. 'Got a horse!'

'Well,' McDonough said, corralling the coins, 'at least I've got me a stake until I can land somewheres else.'

Adele returned with a tray of food and set it on the table. She didn't say anything, and for that McDonough was grateful. He felt a little foolish about Helen, letting her sultry beauty cloud his judgement. He had needed the job when he first hit town, but the girl had wanted more than a hired hand, and he had known that from the beginning.

After breakfast, McDonough and Adele stood at the

door for a long moment, saying nothing, drinking in each other's image. Then he turned and walked out into the street. Thackery was there talking to an excited shop-keeper.

'What is it?' McDonough asked.

'Another body, and a mule near frozen to death in an alley.'

CHAPTER NINE

They found the body stuffed in a tool-shed off of Butte Street, a hundred feet from Danvers' Retreat. The two men looked darkly at the saloon.

'That's a place you're going to have to clean out one of these days,' McDonough said.

'I know. Of course, you've been picking these rabble off one by one. Maybe I'll just let you finish the job.'

McDonough shook his head. 'Unh-Unh. I've had enough killing. All I wanted was to get warm and find a place to light for the winter. I didn't bargain on this mess.'

Thackery went to the body, pushing through a ring of curious onlookers. The man had been stuffed into the shed roughly and at an awkward angle. Pushing aside fallen shovels and rakes, Thackery pulled the body out onto the snow and into the light. The bearhide coat, the thick, matted beard, told McDonough this was the hermit of the hills.

'One of yours from last night?' Thackery asked.

'Maybe. That's the fella that tried to kill me up in the hills.'

'Saves us a trip.'

McDonough knelt beside the body and opened the heavy coat. The man wore wide suspenders which held up

127

a good but well-worn pair of woolen pants. There was an old Navy Six jammed into his waistband. On several of the unused belt loops were bits of rawhide, knotted with their ends cut. McDonough reached absently for the lump of gold rock in his pocket.

'I was close up there, Thackery,' he told the constable. 'Too close.'

'So, he followed you into town to kill you? Why didn't you see him?'

'He didn't have to follow that closely. Where else was I going to go?'

Thackery nodded. 'You notice the cut strings. Somebody knew about those ... strings.' The constable selected words carefully to keep the full meaning from the gathered crowd. He twice had tried in vain to shoo them away.

'His partner.'

There were three neat holes in Robaire's chest. McDonough closed the coat again and examined the hairy hide. There were three holes in the coat as well, and the hair was singed and black.

'The killer got close,' Thackery said. 'Just like with Gregory.'

'Small gun. Right up to his chest. Wouldn't've made much noise, and the coat would have covered the muzzle flash.'

'From what you've told me, this fella was pretty cagey. Why would he let someone get that close?'

'Maybe he wanted to, or couldn't help himself.'

'What do you mean?'

When McDonough didn't answer, Thackery suggested they go check out the mule. They found it in an alley, standing quietly, shivering. It jumped as the men neared.

Most of the mining-tools that had been tied to the saddle were scattered in the snow. The pack saddle was askew, the cinches having been cut. The saddle bags were open, their contents strewn about, as was the bedroll.

'The dead man's?' Thackery asked. McDonough nodded. 'Whoever killed him was looking for something, and had a strong mad on for it.'

'The killer didn't find anything, I'm sure of it. That old bear wouldn't't've left his stash where it could be found. He kept it on him at all times to guard it.'

'Cost him his life,' Thackery mused. 'How much gold, I wonder, is worth a life.'

'Two lives. Maybe more.' McDonough patted the freezing mule. 'This beast has been poorly used. I'll get it under cover while you finish up.'

'Meet me at the doc's office,' Thackery agreed.

Doctor Cherney had a small house just past the assay office, white with neat green trim. He had Robaire laid out on a table in the front room. To McDonough's surprise, Forester's man Strap Gibson was there, his mouth swollen and dark. The man looked as if he were in a great deal of pain.

'Who is he?' Thackery was demanding of Gibson as McDonough entered. He shoved Gibson against the table on which the dead man lay.

'Don't know.' Gibson stared away from the corpse, not blinking. 'Never saw him.'

With a violent thrust Thackery grabbed Gibson's hair and twisted his head toward Robaire's body.

'Maybe now that you're looking at him you'll be able to tell.'

Wrenching free, Gibson mumbled painfully: 'Told you. Never saw him.'

'Yeah. That's what you told me.' Thackery turned to the doctor. 'Gibson said he had an early appointment, Doc. That true?' he asked.

'Yes. He came in early this morning. That *accident* sure did a number on his jaw. Lucky it wasn't broken clean off.'

'Yeah,' Gibson mumbled, glaring at McDonough. 'Lucky.'

'OK, Doc. He's all yours. Good luck, Gibson.'

Outside, McDonough stopped Thackery.

'What was that about?'

'Thought maybe Gibson had done the killing.'

McDonough said no. 'He carries a forty-four. He could have another gun, but he didn't kill the French miner.'

'He knew him, though.' McDonough agreed. Gibson was a poor liar. 'And he might have been behind the attack on you. He hates you enough.'

'You and me both, now,' he told the constable with a grin.

'Let's go see Forester. I want to see what he knows about this gold.'

'That reminds me,' McDonough said, taking the nugget out of his pocket. 'I saw an assay office. I want to stop there and check out the rock I'm carrying around. The assayer might know if more of it was found recently.'

'Pickney doesn't come in but once or twice a week now, and that only to give haircuts.'

McDonough laughed. 'He's the barber, too?'

'Well, he ain't much of one, but he's all we've got.'

'Let's roust him, then.'

'No, I want to see Forester. If you knew about the miner Forester might have, too. Little gets by him in this part of the country, especially when it affects him.'

From the window of Doctor Cherney's house Gibson watched as the two men talked in the street. Hatred played openly on his face. He had drawn his revolver and held it with agitated fingers, slowly spinning the cylinder. Click. Click. Click. When the two men turned and went to the stable for their horses, Gibson made a decision.

The air had warmed considerably as a bright sun coursed through empty blue sky. The two men opened their coats and eventually took them off, tying them to the backs of their saddles before arriving at Forester's ranch. They passed under the wooden arch and into a yard full of activity. A dozen men were loading bales of hay and horses were being hitched up to a string of flatbed wagons. No one paid McDonough or Thackery any attention as they dismounted at the main house and crossed the wide veranda to the front door.

'What do you two want?' Forester said, coming to the door. He carried a sheaf of papers in his hand, studying them without looking up as he spoke.

'We need to talk,' Thackery said.

'I don't have time for you.' Forester stepped out onto the veranda and called to one of the men. 'Where's Gibson?'

'Went to town last night for the doctor,' came the reply.

Forester grumbled beneath his breath, shooting a hot look at McDonough.

'Well, you come here, Thompson,' he said, 'and show these men off my land.'

Thompson started toward the house. Thackery held up a hand, stopping the man.

'We're not leaving, Mr Forester. Official police business.'

Forester edged close to Thackery, fury boiling inside him.

131

'I've got official business, too, Nels. I've got five thousand head of cattle haven't eaten much in days and need to be fed. Now that the weather's breaking I aim to do just that.'

Thackery had to tilt his head back to look Forester in the eye.

'After we're done with our talk,' he said, calmly.

The rancher took a long slow breath then turned and went back into the house. Thackery and McDonough followed. They found the man in the dining-room, already seated, going over his papers as if the other men didn't exist.

'Should have let you sit in jail,' Forester said after a time. Glancing up from his work he asked McDonough: 'This is trouble you're bringing, isn't it?'

McDonough shrugged and tried to force a grin.

'I don't like it any more than you do, Mr Forester. I didn't ask for this trouble.'

'But it finds you, doesn't it? And you just have to kill or bust things up to make it stop.'

'I only came to this country looking for shelter. Not a fight.'

'Men like you don't have to look for trouble. I've seen your kind. They tear apart a land, stir everything up until lead starts flying. We had our share of trouble in the old days. I think it's best if you take yours and leave.'

'You're wrong about me, Mr Forester.'

'He can't leave just yet, Forester,' Thackery said. 'Not now. Men are dead. More men in town last night.'

Forester's face darkened. 'I've got nothing to do with it. I saw right off McDonough wasn't the man I hated and I haven't bothered him since.'

'Not saying you did. But I have some questions, none

the less. And some things to say.'

'Then say them, blast you, and let me get on with my business.'

Thackery pulled a chair out from the table and sat.

'Do you know of anyone living up in the hills?'

Forester was clearly shocked by the question.

'Who would live out there? That's crazy.'

'You told me you thought Gregory had a partner lived up in those hills,' said McDonough.

'Sure, they were stealing cattle. I caught him at it. But I don't figure this partner would stay around if Gregory were out of the picture. Just who is this man?' Thackery described Robaire. 'Never saw him. Bring him out here and let me talk to him.'

'He was murdered in town last night,' McDonough said. 'He'd come into town to kill me. We think he was a miner working a claim up in the hills, and he was sure ready to kill to keep it hidden. He almost got me a couple of days ago when I was trailing him.'

Stunned, Forester stared at the two men. Then his face exploded with laughter and he slapped the table with the palm of his hand. The sound was like thunder.

'You're a fool! Both of you. Nels, I'm surprised at you. You know the gold was played out of those hills ages ago.'

'Sprigensguth started as a boom town, didn't it,' McDonough observed.

'Yeah. But some of us saw potential beyond that blamed yellow rock and stayed after the gold-diggers moved on. We built something they never could, something lasting. We've had two booms, mister, and neither one brought out more than a few thousand in gold.'

McDonough pulled the gold nugget out of his pocket and dropped it on the table. Forester looked it over for a minute before picking it up and rubbing his fingers over the dull yellow pieces embedded in the stone.

'There's more of it, of that I'm sure. The dead man had at least three bags tied to his pants when he was killed. Maybe more.'

Forester no longer wore a belligerent expression. His face was creased with worry.

'You figure Gregory was really after gold?'

'That's what I'm thinking.'

'Don't understand the cattle-rustling, though,' Thackery said, wonderingly.

'Greed,' Forester told him, now sullen and quiet. He looked as if he had been compressed by some great hand pushing down on him. 'Blasted greed can take over any man, if it's what he wants.' They watched Forester as the man's eyes searched the table in front of him for some answers. But there was nothing written on the polished wood, only a slightly distorted image of himself staring back at him. 'Can you find this place in the hills where you had your run in with this fellow?' he asked and McDonough nodded.

'Where is it?'

'Near as I can figure, it's on your land.'

They rode for nearly an hour before reaching the low foothills. Forester led, his lean mustang fidgeting with the desire to run. The air had warmed considerably and the snow was visibly melting, creating slushy puddles here and there. Tufts of yellowish grass peaked out from beneath the sagging blanket of snow. Spring was still a month off, but the land seemed as fidgety as Forester's mustang, ready to bust out with renewed life.

The two men looked at McDonough expectantly.

'That way,' he told them, pointing toward a fold in the wooded hills where he thought he recognized an outcropping of limestone.

Shadows fell across them as they worked their way between the hills for another hour. The horses stumbled and slipped on slick rocks. The going was treacherous and the men wobbled in their saddles.

Without warning, a rifle shot cracked in the narrow canyon and in that same instant Thackery yelled and fell from his horse. With no room to turn, McDonough and Forester threw themselves out of their saddles as bullets buzzed over their heads.

'Where is he?' Thackery asked weakly, cradling his shoulder while trying to pull out his gun.

'Never mind. Let's get up into those trees,' McDonough said. 'Hurry.'

McDonough lifted the wounded constable and, arm wrapped around the man's waist, ran up the hill. Forester had managed to pull his long gun with him as he dropped from his horse and now covered their retreat with wildly aimed shots. Return fire churned up snow at his feet and smacked into tree-trunks as he ran for cover with the others behind some deadfall.

Shivering, Thackery pulled out his six-gun.

'Hold on there, lawdog,' McDonough said, with a grin. 'Whyn't you let us handle this.'

'You ain't the one he shot!'

'This is another of your blamed enemies, McDonough. Bad enough they want you dead, but they aim to get all of us now.'

'Are we still on your land, Mr Forester?' McDonough had helped Thackery remove his arm from his shirtsleeve. The bullet hadn't gone into the arm, only grazed the skin.

Still, blood flowed profusely.

'Yes. We are,' Forester said.

'Then he's your enemy, not mine.'

Thackery gasped as McDonough packed snow onto the wound and held it there until it turned red. The constable stopped him as he reached for another handful of clean snow.

'I've got it,' Thackery said.

Turning to Forester, McDonough said: 'That's the other partner out there.'

'The boss of this thing?'

McDonough got a far away look in his eyes. 'No. That's someone else. Someone who has the strength to control all these men.'

'You seem blamed sure of yourself,' Forester rumbled.

'I am now.'

McDonough shifted away from the protective deadfall, sliding downhill a bit. No other shots had come since they had gotten under cover. Keeping low, Forester slid down beside him.

'He's up in that limestone outcropping,' said McDonough, pointing. 'I saw the muzzle flash.'

'He wouldn't stay there now.'

'I think he would. From there he could cover a lot of ground.'

'We'll go around him.'

'And he'll pick us off from behind. He knows where we're going.'

Forester shook his head. 'That's crazy. Who would know we would come out here?'

'Someone who knows you,' McDonough said gravely.

'No. I don't believe it.'

Looking down the hill McDonough saw a low rock sticking out of the snow. 'Get to that cover and keep the shooter busy for a while.'

'And you?'

'I'm going to circle around, get him from behind.' He checked the loads in his gun.

Turning to leave, Forester laid a heavy hand on McDonough's shoulder. There was something dark in his eyes, and something sad, too.

'Don't kill him,' the rancher said, his voice soft, almost pleading. 'I want to talk to him, so don't kill him.'

'That's up to him.'

Up at the deadfall, Thackery stopped him.

'Bring me back a prisoner, not a corpse.'

Crouching, McDonough made his way uphill, dodging around tall spruce and the occasional cottonwood to the sporadic sound of Forester's rifle fire. He was beyond view of the limestone rock now and wasted no time cresting the hill. Snow deadened his footsteps. He had gone 200 feet along the ridge when he stopped and peaked over the hill-top. To his right was a large, lone oak growing on a slant out of a round rock on the downslope. McDonough could see the top of the leafless tree and part of its trunk. This was a landmark he had seen earlier and it sat directly above the limestone outcropping where the shooter hid. A man lay in a cut in the rock; a rifle barrel and a gray hat were clearly visible from above.

Forester kept up his fire, his bullets sparking off rock or whining through the trees. The bushwhacker was cagier, holding his fire for a clear shot.

McDonough holstered his Remington and moved around the oak. For a few minutes he lost sight of the man in the rocks as he climbed out onto a snow-covered ledge. Not much wider than a game trail, the ledge wound around a boulder out of sight. For a long moment McDonough watched, sensing no movement and seeing no shadows lurking.

Easing around the corner, Remington again in hand, McDonough braced for a gunshot. None came. And the man was gone.

McDonough was above the cut by a few feet. He looked out to where Forester had hidden himself, praying the rancher wouldn't mistake him for the shooter. His first instinct was to look up along the ragged cliff above the boulders. Seeing nothing, he stepped down into the cut and followed it out to the edge where it fell off in a gentle slope to the bottom of the hill.

The man had disappeared.

'Forester,' McDonough called, holding his arms up, waving them.

Suddenly the rancher stood, leveled his rifle, and fired two snap shots. Bullets buzzed angrily past McDonough's head even before he could move. He heard a grunt from behind him and the sick slapping sound of bullets smashing into flesh.

He spun round and saw a man on the far side of one of the boulders slip below sight, his rifle twirling up into the air. McDonough threw himself toward the man, missed grabbing his hand by inches, and watched the body slide down into the fold of the narrow canyon below.

At the bottom of the hill he found the man face down and turned him over. It was Gibson. The man had a bloody hole in his chest and another in his gut. Already his eyes were glazing and although his face was lathered in sweat he shivered violently.

Forester ran up and fell to his knees beside his foreman, roughly shoving McDonough aside. He scooped the man up into his arms, tears welling in his eyes.

'Why, Gibson?' the rancher asked, looking suddenly older.

With a sickly grin, Gibson whispered; 'Gold,' then slumped in Forester's arms. Thackery stumbled down the hill, and ran up to the men. He stood for a time, quiet, letting Forester have a private moment with Gibson.

'He was like a son to me,' Forester mumbled weakly. 'If I had ever bothered to be a father. Why would he do this?'

'Greed,' McDonough said, echoing Forester's own words. The rancher glared up at him, blaming him with blind hatred. But the emotion passed quickly. Forester was no fool, even in his grief, and he had never been one to eschew the truth.

'He would have had it all soon enough,' Forester said, looking down again at Gibson, so peaceful in death.

'For some men tomorrow is never soon enough.'

Thackery didn't put up a fuss when Forester insisted on taking Gibson back to the ranch to be buried. They found Gibson's horse and slung his body over the saddle. The saddle bags were empty, but McDonough hadn't expected to find any gold in them. Together they rode out of the hills then watched as Forester trudged back toward his ranch leading Gibson's horse.

'He hates you, you know,' Thackery said. 'Probably always will.'

McDonough nodded sadly. 'But he doesn't blame me. He knows I didn't set any of this in motion. He blames himself for not seeing it first, and stopping it. Come on. Let's get you patched up.'

It was midday when they got back into Sprigensguth. The town had come alive now that the weather was warming. The streets were muddy and had been gouged by wagon wheels and horses. Snow still clung to the sides of the street and along the base of the boardwalks.

As they rode toward the far end of Main Street another rider was coming into town trailing a gray horse. It was Sven. Thackery stopped outside Doctor Cherney's house and dismounted, pain twisting his face. McDonough stayed aboard the roan and waited until Sven finished looping the gray's reins over the hitching post.

Sven shook his head sadly.

'You had it good there. Vork, good food, and she like you. I'm glad she kick you out.'

'No you're not, kid.'

'I think you cause trouble for her like Gregory.'

McDonough grinned. 'Not exactly like him. I don't have any holes in me yet.'

'Goodbye, McDonough.'

'Sven! Don't go just yet.' The boy paused, twisting around in the saddle. 'I want you to stay in town for a day or two. At least until the trouble's taken care of.'

'Troubles are all gone now,' he said. 'You're off the Box-J.'

Spurring his horse, Sven galloped out of town.

Half an hour later Thackery stepped out of the doctor's office flexing his shoulder and grimacing.

'Miserable old coot wouldn't give me anything for the pain but laudanum,' the constable complained. 'A drink'd do more for me.'

'Later. I sent word to the assayer I needed a haircut.'

Pickney was a wiry man of about fifty who looked lost inside his own clothing. His bald pate, ringed with choppy gray hair, didn't offer positive testament to his skill as a barber. He jumped up from his chair as McDonough and

Thackery entered, a bell tinkling over their heads. He started at the sight of the sombrero but recovered quickly.

McDonough wasted no time on pleasantries. He drew his Remington and stuck the muzzle on the end of Pickney's nose. The man went cross-eyed looking at the thing.

'What – what. . . ?' Pickney stammered in a reedy voice.

'We don't want haircuts, Pickney. We want you to talk.'

Digging the gold rock out of his pocket McDonough tossed it onto a table next to the chair. It pinged as it bounced on a small metal tray. He waggled the gun slightly.

'Take a look, Pickney,' he commanded.

Trembling, the man turned his head away from the gun and looked at the rock. He didn't have to pick it up to recognize it.

'It's gold, gentlemen,' he said, his voice quivering. 'I congratulate you.'

'You've seen it before, Pickney. Recently. Someone brought a bag of it in for you to analyze.'

'I'm sure I don't . . .' Pickney froze as he felt McDonough's gun barrel in his ear.

'You were saying.'

'Constable Thackery, will you allow this brutish behavior to continue?'

'Pickney, you're a greedy little jackal,' Thackery said as he pushed McDonough's gun arm down. 'There's something rotten in town and it's all centering around this gold. Men are dead. More might be killed. I need to know what's going on.'

Glancing fearfully at McDonough, Pickney trembled and slumped into his chair. 'I was brought a bag of gold two months ago. I tested it and, of course, it was real.

141

Nothing looks quite like gold. I was very excited and planned to start mining again myself. I thought the hills had been played out. But I was promised an equal cut of whatever was found if I didn't let word out that gold had again been discovered. It was quite harmless, really, and easier than digging myself. I was brought three more bags over the past few weeks, all of them peppered with gold.'

'How much?'

'I never saw the vein, but from its description and the samples I had been shown, I believe the strike would net more than fifty thousand dollars.'

'So who brought in the gold to be tested?'

Pickney hesitated.

'Helen,' said McDonough. His back was rigid and his voice stiff as he spoke.

Pickney nodded vigorously, confused.

'That's right. How did you know?'

'I'm curious about that myself,' Thackery said.

'I'll explain later,' McDonough answered, scooping up the gold rock. 'We need to ride.'

Scowling, Thackery shrugged.

'I guess that drink will have to wait.'

They rode in silence following a wagon road south out of town, muddy ruts edging up through the slushy snow. Thackery knew immediately their destination and shot a glance over at McDonough. The man sat the roan grimly determined, eyes locked on the horizon, jaw rigid. A thousand questions peppered the constable's mind, but he knew instinctively to let this man alone. At least for the time being.

Night was falling – a blood-red glow shot through with scraps of gray and blue and orange painted the western

142

sky. Eventually they paused atop a low mound and looked down at the Box-J. A single light was on in the main house and the cookhouse was lit with a cooking-fire, but the rest appeared empty and silent.

They entered the yard at a walk and swung down outside the cookhouse. Thackery started to pull his long gun from its boot then thought better of it. When he looked up he saw McDonough eyeing him.

'I was thinking of Sven,' the constable said with an apologetic shrug.

'You won't need it for him either.'

'He'll protect her.'

'He'll try.'

A noise prompted McDonough to spin, lifting the Remington in the same smooth action. Sarah yelped seeing the gun and instinctively shrank in the doorway.

'Mr McDonough!' she scolded.

A little embarrassed, he lowered the gun.

'What ever are you pulling a gun on me for?'

McDonough stepped close to her.

'Where's Helen?'

The old black woman became instantly suspicious, and protective. Eyes narrowed, she turned to Thackery.

'She's not here.'

'Where'd she go?'

'Don't know.' She shrugged.

McDonough turned back to the yard, sweeping his gaze over the barn and the house, both of which now lay under a blanket of darkness.

'And Sven?' he asked.

'Lit out after her when he got back,' she answered, coldly.

Thackery turned for the horses.

'Thank you, Sarah,' he said.

'Hold up,' McDonough said. 'It won't be safe to track them at night. We'll go in the morning.'

Thackery thought for a moment, reluctant, but he agreed.

'I expect you men would like some supper, then? Put up your horses and wash before you come to my table.'

They found plates overflowing with steak, a pan of cornbread, and a heavy blue coffee-pot sitting on the table when they returned. Wasting no time, the men ate.

'Miss Helen's in trouble, isn't she, Mr Thackery.'

'Yes, Sarah.'

'That poor girl. Wanting so much. Her not able to get it.'

The old cook went to the end to the table and sat. She poured herself a cup of coffee and stared at the steam rising.

'Reckon I should move on,' she said, wistfully. 'But I won't leave that child alone. Been with her too long. Wiped her nose and dried her tears, even tanned her hide a time or two when her father weren't around to do it proper. No, sir, I won't leave her.'

Sopping up gravy, Thackery asked:

'She having trouble with the ranch?'

'Been trouble near as long as I knowed this family. Her father weren't much of a businessman. Still, he got by. Helen never could get a foothold once he passed. And the men! Weren't a one of them worth his salt. Either wanting her or wanting the land, or both. But always taking. She wanted to make something of this place. Could have, too, but the wrong sort always crawled out from under the next rock.' This last she said directed toward McDonough with a venomous stare.

'I wanted nothing from her, Sarah. Just a place to work for the winter.'

'And you was the first,' Sarah said, nodding. 'The first man not looking for quick riches or an easy woman. That's why she fell in love with you.'

'She wasn't in love, Sarah. Maybe she thought she was. She certainly wanted me to think so. But she was too clumsy at it, too desperate. What she wanted was someone she could control. Like she controlled Gregory and Gibson.'

Sarah spat on the floor.

'She never controlled Gregory. He was a vile one. Would have hurt her, too, until I showed him my shotgun and that I could use it.'

The old cook shook her head, laughing silently. Then a tear fell and she quickly brushed it away.

'She killed Gregory, Sarah.'

She was quiet for a long time before she whispered: 'I expect I knew that.'

After dinner they went into the main house.

'I'll be going to my room,' Sarah said. 'I'll be up for you gentlemen in the morning and get you breakfast.'

'Thank you, Sarah,' Thackery said, watching her go.

McDonough said nothing, but when she paused half-way down the hallway and looked back, he held her dark eyes with his own. Sarah was a strong woman, and a proud one. Yet now she was begging him, pleading for Helen's life. He didn't know how to tell her that it wasn't up to him. It was Helen's decision or the law's, and all he could do was to see that she did no more harm.

CHAPTER TEN

'You were pretty rough on her,' Thackery said after Sarah had closed her door. He had brought the coffee-pot in with them and was pouring the last of it into his cup. 'You sure Helen killed Gregory?'

McDonough nodded. 'And that old goat in the bearskins, too.' He was suddenly edgy, needing to move. He paced for a moment then strode toward the back of the house to a small, plain bedroom. There were no feminine frills here, only a stout bed, a four-drawer dresser, a wash-stand, and a chair. The only nod to a woman's presence was a bright, pleated set of curtains hanging over the window and a round vanity mirror standing on a small table by the chair.

Impatiently, McDonough fingered the few items on top of the table then rifled through the drawer's contents of kerchiefs and undergarments. He lifted the mattress and pulled the pillow out of its case. Then he turned to the dresser and roughly searched through the drawers.

'No call for that, McDonough,' the constable said, rushing into the room.

He ignored the lawman. In the third drawer he found a canvas bag about the size of his fist, the mouth of it drawn tightly by a plain string. He loosened the string and poured gold-flecked rocks into his hand and showed Thackery. Handing these to the constable he continued his search until he uncovered a red silk kerchief bundled and double-knotted at the bottom of a drawer. Opening it he found a small gold locket that had been damaged. It was dented and slightly twisted. Inside was the photograph of a woman behind a cracked oval of thin glass. As he handled it, the glass fell into pieces, as did the locket.

'Pretty woman,' Thackery said.

McDonough felt as if he were intruding and tried to put the locket-pieces back together. Something caught his eye and he felt his heart jump a bit. He turned the oval-shaped photograph over to find an inscription on the back.

'Clara Merschaux,' Thackery read. 'San Francisco. Is that your Clara?'

'Gregory's.'

Thackery fingered the locket touching some dark spots on the dulled rim.

'Blood,' he announced.

'Probably.'

The two men returned to the main room and sank heavily into chairs, each deep in his own thoughts.

'So how do you figure this?' Thackery asked at last. 'Why Helen?'

'Sarah told us tonight why, and Helen told me much the same thing when I first started working here, although not in so many words. She was desperate. Things were bad and she needed to hold onto the ranch.'

'But murder?'

'I don't think it came easily. Other things worked better for her. She liked to use men. She was good at it. You've seen how Sven follows her like a puppy. She tried that on me.'

'I guess you're too tough, huh?'

McDonough grinned. 'Not so tough. But my mind was . . . elsewhere. Gregory was the one she latched onto, but in the end I don't think she could control him.'

'Because she fired him,' Thackery said.

'No, I don't think so. That was part of her plan. She wanted someone in Forester's camp to keep tabs on him. She didn't want Forester finding out about the gold.'

'Then why kill him?'

'Greed. His probably, not hers. He had tried to pad his earnings by stealing cattle and got caught. It was too dangerous to let him live. Or maybe it was about jealousy. She could have found out about girls in town he frequented, or about Clara. She didn't take that locket just so she could write Clara and confess.'

'I don't know, Rafe,' the constable said, shaking his head. 'It could've been Sven. And for the same motive: jealousy.'

'Sure. Sven and Gregory did have a run-in. It was some time after Gregory had gone to work for Forester. Apparently he had come back to the Box-J and Sven chased him off.'

'He tell you this?'

'No. When I first got here he belted me.' McDonough laughed, rubbing his jaw lightly. 'He said something like: "I told you to stay away". He thought I was Gregory, just like everyone else did.'

'And he didn't know Gregory was dead.'

'He didn't.'

'What about the Frenchman?'

'I don't exactly know how he fit in. She may have found him, or he found her. Maybe he knew her father. Doesn't matter, really. He was the one doing the digging and figured he had a lot to lose so he followed me into town to kill me.'

'You think Helen killed him, too?'

'Had to've. It was the same caliber gun that was used to kill Gregory.'

'You sure it was her gun?'

'We'll know when we find her, but I know she uses a Colt Rainmaker. It's a thirty-two. I've seen her use it. She's good.' Pacing, he thought for a time before outlining his ideas. 'I had been missing for a couple of days and that probably worried her. She came riding in at night – maybe looking for me or to meet Gibson – and when she saw the miner in town she decided to get rid of another problem.'

Thackery got up and nursed the fire for a bit, throwing another log on.

'That's cold-blooded, Rafe. Especially for a woman.' McDonough nodded. 'So you figure Gregory got beat up by Gibson when he was caught rustling, then Forester gave him the boot, telling him to get out of the country. Only he came back here to talk to Helen and got shooed away by Sven.'

'Yes. But not before talking to Helen. She made plans to meet him. That's why he let his killer get so close. He was expecting a kiss and a warm embrace. Instead he got four slugs.'

'OK, what about Gibson?'

'Ace in the hole, I guess. Or maybe he put things together after Gregory was dead and dealt himself in. He was greedy, too. Forester called that one. Think about it. He'd get Forester's land, the gold, and a beautiful woman with her own spread. He'd control virtually the entire south valley. That's a lot to lose and he wouldn't give it up without a fight. I'm sure he's the one tried to kill me the other night in that shed. And let's not forget that he lied to us about when he'd gotten to town.'

Thackery grunted with disgust as he flopped back in his chair.

'The whole blamed town is rotten. It makes me sick.'

'Not all of it, Nels. Just a few stupid, greedy people.'

'Yeah, but they're almost all gone now, aren't they?'

'Tomorrow. One way or another, they'll all be gone tomorrow.'

McDonough took the lead the following morning, letting the roan find its way back into the hills. They had left Sarah behind crying, a lie in her ears. McDonough had told her that he'd bring Helen back; that she wasn't too far gone yet. The words had left a knot in his gut.

Without a word, each man withdrew his long gun and laid it across his saddle. They hadn't spoken to one another since last night, the light breeze whispering across the plains the only sound in their ears. But now, climbing their way into the hills, the silence seemed deafening.

At each ridge they paused and, using trees or rocks for cover, peered cautiously over the hilltop. The tracks they followed came and went, sometimes in snow, sometimes sunken deeply in new mud. Helen wasn't covering her backtrail. She was running. Wherever the gold had been hidden she was hurrying to retrieve it.

Thackery tapped him on the shoulder and pointed toward a gully where a brown gelding lay in the mud. Sven's pony. The animal was still kicking weakly with one leg when they reached it, and shivering violently. Two of its legs had been broken, the bones jabbing out of the animal's skin. The mud told the story of how the pony had slipped, lost its footing, and tumbled down the side of the hill.

Pulling his revolver, Thackery took aim at the pony's head. McDonough put a hand out to stop him. He shook his head warningly. For an instant the constable hated McDonough for his cool cruelty. But the man made no apology, and Thackery knew he was right. A shot would warn Helen that they were closing in. McDonough lead the roan up the hill. Thackery hesitated, casting a backward glance at the suffering animal before following. At the top of the hill he looked back and saw that the pony had finally stopped moving.

Passing through a stand of aspen McDonough stopped, seeing something flapping in the breeze. The familiar image sent a chill through his bones. Hanging from a low, bare branch was a hat, a white Stetson, weathered and soiled and with a crooked crease down the middle. It was Sven's hat, and it was streaked with blood.

They searched but couldn't find Sven's body. McDonough found spots of blood and places where Sven had fallen to his knees and then onto his back. From there, the horse-tracks continued out of the stand and so did Sven's bootprints. Despite injury, he continued to follow her, stumbling, sometimes crawling to keep up.

'The blasted fool,' McDonough cursed violently.

Late afternoon they found themselves outside a wide-mouthed cavern. They left their horses out of sight, then divided their approach, creeping up to it from opposite sides. McDonough entered first, eyes squinting against the darkness. Cautiously he lit a match and from that meager light found a lantern. There wasn't much to see inside. It wasn't deep and it wasn't wide. A straw bed had been made for an animal, and another had been made for a man. There was a firepit, now cold, a coffee-pot, a satchel with jerky and moldy biscuits. Beneath the bedroll lay a weather-beaten, dog-eared Bible.

'Our dead miner's home sweet home,' Thackery said.

Coming out of the cave they saw where the tracks wound through the trees and passed over the next hill.

'It's going to be dark soon,' Thackery said, glancing up at the purpling sky. 'We'll need to find shelter. This cave will do.'

McDonough stared at the tracks, unblinking.

'They can't be far. We need to finish this.'

Thackery suddenly grabbed hold of McDonough's arm and spun him, taking hold of both shoulders and shaking.

'You've got thoughts of vengeance in you, Rafe,' the constable snapped. 'I won't have it. Do you hear? I'll place her under arrest, she'll be tried. That's all we can do.' McDonough's eyes were hot pokers; his jaw tight as a whiskey-drum as he strained desperately against his own violent emotions. 'Tell me now, Rafe. Did you know Gregory? Or the miner?'

'Never saw either of them before in my life,' McDonough said, tightly. 'They were no friends and no kin.'

'Then why. . . ?'

'She murdered Gregory, Nels, and left him to die alone and freezing, with no one to know of his passing. I can't explain it.'

Thackery released him and stepped back. A look of sadness worked into his face.

'You liked her, didn't you,' he said quietly.

McDonough's jaw rippled with anger and he brought a fist up, flexing it. Then he deflated, and the bitter look in his eyes was replaced by resignation.

'Yeah. I did. She's a fiery woman, Nels. A man alone as long as I am wants that in a woman when he comes to town. He wants desire and abandon, and that was Helen. And for a moment I was blinded by it.'

'Just for a moment, friend,' Thackery said, grinning. 'I figure you got your head screwed on straight right around the time you started seeing Adele. No need to be embarrassed.'

'It's not embarrassment. I'm ashamed. She's bad, Nels.'

The constable nodded. 'Yup. That's why I'm going to arrest her. Come on. Let's finish this.'

They heard the sound as they came over the next hill. Metal striking rock. It was muffled and distant, as if it came from deep within the earth, and it echoed around them making it impossible to locate its source. They split up and rode down into an empty hollow, eyes sweeping the tree-lined hills. Thackery spotted it first and waved his arms to catch McDonough's attention.

Half-way up a rocky slope there was a broken overhang that partly hid the entrance to a cave. Several boulders were piled up in front of the opening as well. If it hadn't been for the sounds emanating from within, Thackery would have missed it.

Leaving long guns behind, the two men climbed the boulders to a shattered ledge of shale and sandstone. McDonough drew his Remington, glanced over to Thackery, who had lifted his Colt, then stepped into the black cave.

Inside, the pounding became louder. As their eyes adjusted they could see shapes forming in the dank shadows made by lantern-light reflecting deep from within the narrow cave, long shadows that played on the rugged walls. Rough-hewn timbers, straining to hold back the mountain, had been wedged up against the ceiling forming a lopsided threshold every dozen feet.

The tunnel curved like a snake, and the narrow walls pressed in on them as the two men quietly worked their way deeper. Thackery had taken the lead and occasionally had to restrain McDonough from rushing forward. At last he pointed to a corner just ahead. Beyond it the light was brighter and the sound of digging was stronger. They heard voices.

'Please,' Sven's voice whimpered. 'I need to rest.'

'Shut up!' A slap echoed in the cave.

They could hear Sven cry out then breathe rapidly in shallow, ragged gasps.

'Oh, darling,' Helen cooed. 'I'm sorry. I know you're hurt, but just a little more. Then we'll be together.'

Thackery stepped around the corner, gun leveled.

'Drop it, Helen.'

They were in a wide spot perhaps fifteen feet across. Three lanterns hanging on the wall formed a jaundiced circle of light. Beyond them, the tunnel continued into a Stygian gloom. Helen was crouched beside Sven who had fallen to his knees. He was stripped to the waist and blood streaked down his face and onto his chest. His eyes were dull and vacant, his mouth slack. The boy was dead on his feet. He held a pickaxe loosely in one hand. Behind him the rock he had been digging was chipped and gouged with blows from the heavy tool, and beside him, at Helen's feet, were seven fist-sized burlap sacks bulging with gold. There were several thick veins of the stuff worked through the rock like the streaks of blood on Sven's head and chest.

Slowly, Helen stood but her gun hand remained lowered, the muzzle pointing at the back of Sven's head. She smiled oddly, seeing McDonough come around the corner.

'Rafe,' she said, a sweeping lock of her long golden-brown hair masking part of her face. 'Don't be jealous.'

'Put the gun down.' Thackery said. 'The boy needs a doctor.'

'I wish you hadn't come, Rafe,' she said bitterly, sadly. 'I might have been able to persuade the constable to let me finish. He might have even helped me.'

'Then you would have killed him,' McDonough said.

Ignoring him, she said: 'But not you, Rafe. I couldn't sway you, could I.'

'No.'

'We found the locket, Helen,' Thackery said. He had taken three short steps toward her. Still she had not looked away from McDonough.

'Searching through a woman's private things? Not the gentleman I took you for. But then again, I'm not the lady you thought I was.'

Sven moaned and fell forward.

'Let me go to the boy, Helen. He's hurt.'

She turned an evil face to Thackery.

'I know he's hurt, damn you!' she screamed. Her gun came up sharply and she snapped off one shot that ricocheted in the tight cave. Thackery ducked and fell back behind the corner, stone splinters showering him.

McDonough cocked his gun.

'That's enough!'

'No. The ranch is everything to me, Rafe. We could have shared it.'

'Gibson's dead,' he told her coldly.

Her gaze dropped for an instant. Hearing those words, something had gone out of her. She was truly alone now. When she lifted her head again there was a faraway look in her eyes.

'Good,' she said. She leveled her gun at him, the same Colt Rainmaker he had seen her use before, and pulled back the hammer.

'No, Helen!' Sven cried out, jumping to his feet. His weakened body fell against hers, leaden arms reaching up for her throat. A shot cracked, Sven jolted and crumbled to the muddy floor.

Stumbling backwards, Helen fired again, the bullet smacking into a lantern, shattering it and spraying oil fire onto the cavern wall as she disappeared into the unlit portion of the tunnel. Struggling to his feet, Sven followed.

Helen suddenly screamed.

Carrying a lantern with him McDonough found her clinging to a ledge with one hand. Below her was empty blackness. Her knuckles were white and blood trickled from her scraped fingertips as she struggled defiantly. Yet her other hand held fast to a bit of rope to which were tied the seven bags of gold.

'Let it go, Helen,' McDonough said, setting the lantern down. Her hand was six feet below the rim, just out of his reach as he lay prone.

A body slumped down next to McDonough. Breathless and pale, Sven reached over the edge, his long arms stretching out to her. When he grabbed her wrist she yelped in pain and let go of the ledge. For a long moment the two of them hung motionless, Helen dangling over the abyss.

'Good,' she sighed. 'Pull me up.' For a moment, it didn't look like the big Swede would be able to haul her up. Then he found another well of strength and began inching away from the edge.

Helen grinned.

'No, Helen,' Sven cried. McDonough had moved behind Sven, grabbing at the boy's belt loops to pull him back from the hole, when he saw Helen come up over the rim, her Rainmaker searching. 'I won't let you,' the Swede yelled, then lurched forward.

Helen dropped below the rim, screaming. McDonough tumbled forward, his grip torn lose. He fell onto the boy's legs, his weight stopping Sven's slide into the hole.

'Don't, Sven,' Helen begged weakly.

'Come on, boy,' McDonough urged as he tried to pull Sven to safety. The boy's legs had gone stiff. He was fighting against him.

'Helen, I won't let you kill.' Sven's words were distant, his voice trembling. 'Not again.'

With a mighty kick to the head, Sven shoved McDonough off of him and plunged into the abyss. A gunshot echoed alongside a scream. And then silence.

McDonough stared into the blackness for a long minute as he caught his breath. After some time he heard the scrape of a boot and saw light from a lantern approach. Thackery appeared next to him, a knot on his forehead and scrapes all over his face.

'I tried,' McDonough said. Blood trickled down into his eyes from a gash at his temple.

The seven bags of gold rested innocently on a ledge just below the rim of the abyss. With a violent sweep of his hand, McDonough shoved the gold sacks off the ledge and into the black void below.

Thackery nodded.

'I know, Rafe.'

After the spring rains had stopped the wagon roads dried into deeply formed ruts broken only by rows of wild daisies and daffodils. The fields seemed to be full of them, waving in the soft warm breeze and basking in a gloriously warm sun. There was time before summer yet, time to enjoy the sweet air and warm days and still cool nights before the fiery heat of summer settled over the valley in July.

McDonough had yet to see a summer in the valley and he wasn't sure he'd get to. With a new owner taking over the Box-J next week his job as caretaker for the bank-appointed receiver would end. He hadn't made many friends in the valley since his arrival. He didn't know if some outfit would take him on.

Forester might, he thought. He and the old rancher had begun mending fences after Helen's funeral. They would never be fast friends. The old man had lost a lot and blamed himself for it. He blamed McDonough, too, a little, all the while realizing the man had not been the author of his troubles. McDonough understood and didn't press the point. But they had bought each other a drink once, and they had shaken hands. That was enough for now.

Driving in on a springboard, McDonough stopped outside the café. Another wagon was sitting in front of the restaurant and a man was loading boxes into it. Seeing Rafe pull up, Adele came out quickly, wiping her hands on an apron.

'Hello, stranger,' she said with a bright smile.

He stepped down. 'Hello yourself,' he said, pulling her close and kissing her.

'Haven't seen you in weeks.' She wasn't chiding him, he knew, but simply excited to see him.

'Well, the bank's been keeping me busy with the ranch. But that'll end next week.' He looked down at her mean-ingfully, feeling his throat tighten. 'I guess I gotta see about doing something else.'

'You'll land somewhere,' she told him. Her breezy manner caught him off guard. 'Oh, I got a letter for you the other day.' She pulled a plain envelope out of her apron pocket. 'It's from Clara.'

'It came here?'

'Well, we all figured you'd show up here eventually.'

He took the letter and read it.

'She's Gregory's sister,' he told her. 'She doesn't want his things, only the locket.'

'She also thanks you,' Adele said. McDonough noticed that she was beaming but didn't understand why.

'You read it,' he teased. 'Well, I'm not sure she should be thanking me.'

'She knows, Rafe. At least now she knows what happened to him.'

She kissed him again, and suddenly he felt awkward.

'Say, what's going on with the wagon?'

'Packing up. I've closed down the café for a few days until the new owner comes in to take over. I'm done with restaurants, Rafe. I need to move on.'

Stunned, McDonough turned away and leaned against the springboard. He'd felt sure she was waiting for him to finish with the Box-J so they could make plans together. Now she was leaving.

'What about you, Rafe? You have any plans?'

'I guess not. Whoever bought the Box-J will probably have his own crew. I'll be out of a job.'

Adele slipped up behind him, wrapping her arms around his waist.

'Oh, I don't know,' she said. 'You might be able to stay on. That is, if you don't mind working for a woman.'

For a moment he didn't understand her words. Then,

like a light shining in his eyes, he turned around to see her nodding and smiling at him.

'I bought it last week,' she confessed.

'Well, tie me to a hitchin' post!'

'That, Mr McDonough, is the idea.'

Pulling him down to her, she kissed him long and slow. Her fingers played teasingly in his unkempt hair. Then she reached up and pulled his hat from his head and tossed it into the street. Kissing him still, she heard a carriage ride by and out of the corner of her eye saw the sombrero trampled into the dust.